Cornelia

by Mark V. Olsen

A Samuel French Acting Edition

SAMUEL FRENCH

FOUNDED 1830

NEW YORK HOLLYWOOD LONDON TORONTO

SAMUELFRENCH.COM

ISBN 978-0-573-69868-2   Printed in U.S.A.   #29675

MUSIC USE NOTE

Licensees are solely responsible for obtaining formal written permission from copyright owners to use copyrighted music in the performance of this play and are strongly cautioned to do so. If no such permission is obtained by the licensee, then the licensee must use only original music that the licensee owns and controls. Licensees are solely responsible and liable for all music clearances and shall indemnify the copyright owners of the play and their licensing agent, Samuel French, Inc., against any costs, expenses, losses and liabilities arising from the use of music by licensees.

IMPORTANT BILLING AND CREDIT REQUIREMENTS

All producers of *CORNELIA* must give credit to the Author of the Play in all programs distributed in connection with performances of the Play, and in all instances in which the title of the Play appears for the purposes of advertising, publicizing or otherwise exploiting the Play and/or a production. The name of the Author *must* appear on a separate line on which no other name appears, immediately following the title and *must* appear in size of type not less than fifty percent of the size of the title type.

In addition the following credit *must* be given in all programs and publicity information distributed in association with this piece:

World Premiere at The Old Globe, San Diego, California
Louis G. Spisito, Executive Producer

CORNELIA was first produced by Louis G. Spisto at the Old Globe Theatre in San Diego, California on May 16, 2009. The performance was directed by Ethan McSweeny, with sets by John Lee Beatty, costumes by Tracy Christiansen, lighting by Christopher Akerlind, sound by Paul Peterson, and music by Steven Cahill. The production stage manager was Leila Knox. The cast was as follows:

CORNELIA	Melinda Page Hamilton
RUBY	Beth Grant
GEORGE	Robert Foxworth
GERALD	T. Ryder Smith
MARIE	Hollis McCarthy

CHARACTERS

Cornelia...tall, sultry, emotional, early 30s.
Ruby...tall, indominable, loves life, 50s.
George...short, puganious, a fighter, 50s.
Gerald...suspicious, an operator, late 40s.
Marie...simple, decent, loyal 40s.

SETTING

Montgomery, Alabama

TIME

1970-1977; narration is 18 years later.

ACT ONE

(A silver fog swirls. A spot finds **CORNELIA** *centerstage in the mist.)*

CORNELIA. Once upon a time there was a beautiful, magic Kingdom where everything was gorgeous. Where the gentle breezes from the Gulf met the cool air of the Piney Woods and the people doth did prosper. It was fair and just, and liberal and progressive, too. It was a honey of a place and they called it Alabama.

And the Kingdom was ruled by a Royal Family who were beloved by all for their royal ways. And unto the family was born a princess, with eyes blue as the gulf and hair black as a raven's with a zillion little ringlets around her head, and she was so precious they carried her home from the hospital on a satin pillow. And from the very first breath she took – ? She was loved. As if hands had waited all their lives to reach into her crib and scoop her up and adore her, lifting her up unto the sun. When she was 5? She sang "I'm an Old Cow Hand From the Rio Grande," and all the legislators clapped. And she grew to become a grand prix champion, and runner-up Miss Alabama, and a country-western singin' star and THE water Ballet Queen of Cypress Gardens, she truly was. And she dated a real Everly Brother. And everything was gorgeous and perfect.

(A rumble of distant thunder.)

But suddenly, an ill wind blew, and a fever swept the land, and people got mean and brother took to rising up to smite brother, and blood was spilt and the kingdom was torn asunder and the Royal Family was swept aside and did scatter like leaves, fleeing into the darkness, finding safety on the banks of the Pea River, livin' in exile in Elba. Elba, Alabama. Where the Princess grew, livin a life of great obscurity. And she watched. And waited. And remembered. Oh, how she remembered.

(Lights rise on **RUBY***'s front room, a modest home of eccentric taste in unkempt condition.)*

*(***RUBY*** approaches the house with a large box. She wears a white miniskirt and a substantial bandage over the bridge of her nose. She shakes a finger up to what would be the roof:)*

RUBY. You don't fool me – I see you up there.

CORNELIA. Mama – ?!

RUBY. Pigeons nestin' in the eaves. Doin' their business all over my iris.

CORNELIA. Come into the house – it's ten til six – Where the H. have you been – ?!

RUBY. Tag sales. Wait 'til you see these hats! A whole box fulla hats. Fifty cents apiece – Genuine Paris hats – !

*(***CORNELIA*** holds up a dress:)*

RUBY. Nuh-uh, nothin' doin' –

CORNELIA. Mother –

RUBY. No sir, nuh-uh, I hate that dress – I'm wearin' what I got on.

CORNELIA. No, you're not. Miniskirts are not acceptable evening wear. They're inappropriate for a woman of your station, to say nothin' of your girth.

RUBY. That dress makes me look like a big, fat kewpie-doll!

CORNELIA. Jesus, Mother, pinch me raw! I pulled every string in the book to get him over for supper, and you're givin' me nothing but backwash from the get-go. I can name five women in this town who've divorced their husbands just to have a crack at him.

*(***RUBY*** relents and unzips her miniskirt, cataloging her complaints as it falls to the floor:)*

RUBY. "Him." Aaach.

CORNELIA. Here, wear this slip –

RUBY. If he bit hisself he'd need shots for rabies. His hair is oily and greasy. He wears his suits like feedbags –

CORNELIA. *(unbuttoning* RUBY*'s blouse:)* Maybe that's just how I like 'em.

RUBY. That round little face – he's got no chin to speak of.

CORNELIA. And he's twenty years older. Why don't you take him.

RUBY. George Wallace?! He's barely titty high to me.

*(*CORNELIA *groans in a mirror:)*

CORNELIA. These lines around my eyes.

*(*RUBY *groans.)*

CORNELIA. Do I look old? I do, don't I – ? Mother- – ?

*(*CORNELIA *turns:* RUBY*'s pouring a shot of whiskey:)*

CORNELIA. Mother – !

RUBY. I'm thirsty.

CORNELIA. *(grabbing the glass from* RUBY*:)* There's ice water in the kitchen.

RUBY. I can't stand seein' you when you get like this.

CORNELIA. Like what?

RUBY. Sweetie. You're barely home two days and look at you. You're practically throwin' yourself at him. I know this hurts like hell, but this's only your first divorce. I speak from more experience in this area. Divorce hurts, but it's not the end of the world.

CORNELIA. Think he'll like my legs?

RUBY. Honey, once this is finally behind you, we'll hare off on a binge. We'll sell something and go to Atlanta. Or New Orleans. We'll get a hotel room and act goofy. Wouldn't you like that?

(Clicks from WALLACE*'s cleats: he struts toward the house.* CORNELIA *gasps!)*

CORNELIA. That's him – Shoot! I don't even have my eyelashes on –

RUBY. You go on –

(*stepping into the unzipped dress:*)

– I can take care of "him."

CORNELIA. Just don't forget: *you* invited him –

RUBY. (*been over this a million times:*) I know I know I know –

CORNELIA. Talk me up like we said –

RUBY. I know I know I know –

CORNELIA. And he was led to believe we might endorse him for re-election.

(*exit* **CORNELIA.**)

(**RUBY**, *half-way into the dress, grabs the bottle.* **CORNELIA** *sneaks back in:*)

CORNELIA. Mother – !

RUBY. (*startled, overlapping:*) For the love of Mike!

(*They lock eyes:*)

CORNELIA. I'm depending on you.

RUBY. (*releasing the bottle*) O-kay!

(**RUBY** *nods and smiles and watches* **CORNELIA** *exit, then quickly pours a healthy shot. One hand downs the shot, the other holds the dress half up.* **GEORGE WALLACE** *enters, sneaks behind her, poking her in the ribs. She jumps: her drink spills on her slip; her dress falls to the floor:*)

RUBY. Lawd!

WALLACE. Well hello, Miz Ruby!

RUBY. You do that again and I'll bust your nose.

WALLACE. And I'll bust yours back. Oh – I see somebody already has.

RUBY. (*shaking the droplets of whiskey off her slip*) Funny, George. Gimme your handkerchief –

WALLACE. So what the hell you been up to? What's it been, three, four years? Thought maybe you drove off the mountain or dropped dead or sump'n –

RUBY. *(overlapping, re his handkerchief:)* This thing clean – ?

WALLACE. Hey – I just been down in Abbeville, you seen me on TV? Folks love me down there. Shoulda seen that Abbeville crowd, whole town lined up, waitin' hours just to touch me – I mean, they just love me –

(busses her nose:)

So who the hell'd you tangle with this time?

RUBY. None a your business.

(She can't resist:)

Tweetie.

WALLACE. Little Tweetie Thurman?

RUBY. No. Big Tweetie Davis. I will not bring myself to repeat what she called me. She threw her glass across the bar and hit me right here.

(rubs her nose)

It has impaired my thought attempts. I haven't been right since. You can't smell nothin', can you? Smell –

*(**WALLACE** gives her a sniff; rolls his eyes.)*

My daughter'll have a fit – Zip me up –

(turns her back)

She wishes I'd quit high-steppin' – stay home more and just go to church on Sunday, but I just get so bored.

(Fully dressed, with a hat on her head, she turns:)

Now. George Wallace. What are you doin' in my house?

WALLACE. You invited me. Damned near begged.

RUBY. *(cagy:)* Did I?

WALLACE. *(sidles an arm around her:)* Yep. And I thought, why not. I could use me a little pussy.

RUBY. Yeah, me, too. Mine's big as a bucket.

WALLACE. *(laughing)* Goddamn, I've missed you. You haven't changed one bit. I love you, Ruby, I do.

(He tickles her.)

RUBY. *(laughing)* Stop! Stop now, or I swear I'll knock you into the middle of next week n' you better believe it. And we ain't gonna endorse you in the primary, cause I don't like you.

WALLACE. Shore you do.

RUBY. Oh no I don't.

WALLACE. Oh.

(heads to the door:)

Well, see you around sometime –

RUBY. *(cagy, calling after:)* Course – it might be different if someone was to appoint me to somethin' –

(now all charm:)

Care for a drink, George?

WALLACE. You know I don't touch the hard stuff.

RUBY. *(pouring a re-fill)* Any old scrap of a position would do. George, you got so much power you don't know what to do with it. Why don't you gimme a little something to administer?

WALLACE. How 'bout this. How bout, and this is only "if," I get up to Washington and I'm livin' in the White House, and I give you a big office with a view a everything, big desk, big name plaque that says "Miz Ruby – Chairman."

RUBY. A what?

WALLACE. Atomic Energy. I'll put you in charge of all them atom bombs. God, if that ain't fuckin' funny –

(He laughs; she's not amused. He examines photos on the buffet:)

WALLACE. Who's this? This your daughter?

RUBY. I expect so. Cornelia.

WALLACE. Nice teeth.

RUBY. She was 19. In Paris. She was touring with Roy Acuff.

(goading:)

Been to Paris, George?

WALLACE. Hell, I've seen Europe on TV. You can learn as much watchin' TV as you can seein' some teensy automobiles in traffic jams and some decrepit old churches.

(picking up another photo:)

She's damn pretty, Ruby.

RUBY. She's my China Doll.

WALLACE. *(picking up another photo)* This one, too?

RUBY. *(takes the photo and puts it back; warning "off limits":)*

Two years ago. She drove the pace car at the Winston 500 Speedway at Talladega. They're all Cornelia. I'm damn proud of my daughter. She's everything I want my daughter to be. She's smart. She's got good breeding. She's got genuine class.

(CORNELIA *enters; transformed into a stunning vision of loveliness:)*

CORNELIA. Oh Mother. That's so sweet. Governor. Good afternoon.

WALLACE. Howdy. You must be Cornelia. Daughter of Ruby.

CORNELIA. You make the arrangement sound quite biblical.

RUBY. You two sit and I'll check on supper. We're having hot tamales. It's my secret recipe. I call 'em, "Ruby's Awe Shucks."

*(Exit **RUBY**. **CORNELIA** sets down a tray with two glasses and a pitcher of lemonade.)*

WALLACE. *(grinning from ear to ear, extending his hand)*

Pleasure to meet you, Miss Folsom.

CORNELIA. The pleasure's mine. When Mama told me you accepted her invitation, I near fell outta my chair. I'm a great admirer of yours.

WALLACE. Jo'ge.

CORNELIA. Oh and please, you call me Cornelia. Now, I insist.

WALLACE. I was just admiring all your photos – driving race cars and flying jet air planes.

CORNELIA. They say I'm so fast they just might have to put a governor on me.

(*A wonderful moment.*)

WALLACE. How do you suppose it is we never met before?

CORNELIA. (*winking*) I suspect I took the high road and you took the low.

WALLACE. Oh, you don't believe all that junk they say about me.

CORNELIA. I've been gone a long time: what do they say about you?

WALLACE. Mostly what an irresistible devil I am.

CORNELIA. Oh really? Mmmmm. Sit.

(*He sits next to her on the love seat.*)

How's the election coming?

(*He doesn't answer – he's gazing at her.*)

Governor? Your re-election?

WALLACE. Huh – ?

CORNELIA. How come you're grinnin' at me like that?

WALLACE. I feel like I know you. Been home long?

CORNELIA. Two weeks. We do, Darlin.

WALLACE. Beg pardon?

CORNELIA. We do. Know each other. Rather well. You were very married. And I was very single. It was just one of those little one-night things.

(*She shrugs like "no big deal," then lets him squirm.*)

Relax! I was six years old! At a reception in the Mansion when Uncle Jimmy was Governor. I stayed up late hidin' up on the stairs to watch all the dignitaries arrive. You were just elected Circuit Judge. You saw me hidin' and you called me over. You said:

(gruffly:)

CORNELIA. *(cont.)* "Hey, come down here, little girl." And I did. Then you said, "Hey, what's wrong, little giggly-girl? Why you crying?" Well, I said –

(very sweetly:)

"I'm cryin' cause I want to dance, too." And you took my hand and we danced right there in the foyer. To the Tennessee Waltz.

(handing him a glass:)

Lemonade?

WALLACE. Please, Miss Cornelia. Please, Cornelia.

CORNELIA. In Mexico they call it le-mo-nada.

WALLACE. It's very good.

CORNELIA. It's sweet. And it's tart. All at once. It fits most every mood. If I wake up and feel like doing charity at the cancer prevention booth, I put in extra lemon and zip out to the mall and sit behind the table –

(whooping out:)

"Honey, come over here and get your pap smear, right now!" Sometimes I even take a little lemon wedge and wrap it in a napkin and carry it out the door in my purse. That way, if I'm ever caught waiting around somewhere, I just pop that little wedge in my mouth and slip in a little packet of sugar. It's a poor substitute, but (winks) sometimes a girl has to make do. It's all in the balance of the sweet and the sour –

WALLACE. Jesus, I'll tell you this much, you're damn pretty.

CORNELIA. Me? I'm just a rag, a bone and a hank of hair.

(pots and pans crash, off:)

RUBY. *(off)* Oh they fell on the damn floor – !

WALLACE. Do I make you nervous?

CORNELIA. No.

WALLACE. No?

CORNELIA. No.

WALLACE. Oh. It's just that you were lookin' at me funny. Kinda flirty.

(A "gotcha" smirk sweeps his face.)

CORNELIA. Maybe I am a little nervous. I haven't been on many dates, you see. Most of the men in Montgomery fall into one of two unacceptable categories: too young or too married.

WALLACE. Ahhhh. So that's what this's all about –

CORNELIA. Excuse me?

WALLACE. A "date – "

(Caught! She grins; He wags his finger and "tsks.")

WALLACE. Well well well. I'll be damned. So what are you gonna tell your girlfriends about your date?

CORNELIA. I'm havin' a nice time. What will you tell your friends?

WALLACE. *(touching her:)* I'm having a good time, too. I'm startin' to have a real good time.

RUBY. *(appearing briefly in the door:)* Supper's done.

WALLACE. You think you'd be willing to give the guy a second date?

CORNELIA. Perhaps. If he has the time. I know he's in the midst of a very tough re-election.

WALLACE. He can probably find the time.

RUBY. *(off)* Supper! Now!

WALLACE. Later on tonight?

CORNELIA. *(coy)* Can we arrange for a chaperon?

WALLACE. Now what kinda date do you have in mind?

CORNELIA. Ho – Nothin' statutory, I assure you.

*(**WALLACE** whispers into **CORNELIA**'s ear with a grin; she shrieks! with amusement.)*

*(Crossfade to Governor's Mansion. **WALLACE** dashes into the Mansion's first floor: an imposing grand stairwell, Eastlake furniture, etc, as **GERALD**'s on the phone:)*

GERALD. Where'd he go – ?! I need to know where he is –

(half-beat)

Drove himself? He'll run into a truck, he'll run over a baby, he can't drive, he's a terrible driver. You the chauffer, you supposed to chauffer him, now who knows where he's at –

(half-beat)

Because he doesn't know how to use the car phone is why!

(**WALLACE** enters; **GERALD** slams down the phone:)

GERALD. Goddamn you, George! Where the hell you been?! We got rallies in the morning at Auburn, Opelika and Linett – !

MARIE. (off) (calling in:) You want mint in that or just regular?

GERALD. (to **MARIE**) Regular – !

(to **WALLACE**)

– I got half the damn highway patrol sittin on their cans downtown waitin word from you –

WALLACE. For what?

GERALD. Like, how many cars we need, how big an escort, what kinda route you wanna take to Auburn, Opelika and Linett.

WALLACE. (pushing **GERALD** toward the back entry:) Regular number a cars, regular kind a escort, we take the regular route, good night, go home, bye-bye –

GERALD. Whataya talkin' about – ?! We're stayin here tonight.

WALLACE. No you aint –

GERALD. You said we were, you asked us to.

WALLACE. Plans changed. Get your wife and beat it out back –

MARIE. (off) That darn dog got in again. The kitchen door was wide open.

(MARIE enters from the kitchen with two beverages:)

MARIE. *(cont.)* Hello, George. I didn't hear you come in. Something about that dog is not right. Stinks to high heaven, too. P.U. Have a nice night, George?

WALLACE. Yeah, but – sure am tired. Ain't you tired?

MARIE. Not so much.

(sits down to her knitting)

Go on up. You don't have to entertain us.

WALLACE. No, I mean – what I'm sayin' is – I'm just feelin' like, I dunno, I think I just need to be a bit by myself. Alone. Tonight.

MARIE. Oh. Well – alright.

(She collects her things and starts up the stairs –)

WALLACE. No!

MARIE. "No" what?

WALLACE. No that's not what I meant.

MARIE. Well – then, what, then – ?

WALLACE. It's hard to talk about Marie. It's like bein' a little sad – like maybe, I dunno. A little lonely. Empty.

CORNELIA. *(off)* I'm gettin' mighty lonely waitin' out here.

MARIE. Who's that – ?!!

WALLACE. Nobody.

MARIE. Well it is not – !

GERALD. Heh heh heh.

MARIE. *(very disapproving:)* Oh, George –

WALLACE. Now, it's not like you think –

MARIE. This is wrong. This was Lurleen's house. Shame on you.

WALLACE. Now, just – Come here – Look.

*(They peek out at **CORNELIA**:)*

GERALD. Wait a minute – Shit! That's her!

MARIE. Who?

WALLACE. Big Jim's niece.

MARIE. Ruby Folsom Austin's daughter?

GERALD. She's that one I was tellin' you about – !

WALLACE. I met her tonight and said I'd show her the old – momentos.

MARIE. *(dubious as hell:)* What "momentos"?

GERALD. That's the one with Maida Parsons barged their way onto the campaign plane last week, hidin' in back with the press.

WALLACE. You're kiddin' me –

GERALD. Every time I turned around they'd wiggle their way a few seats closer to the front. She raised a holy fit when I told em to drag their butts off –

WALLACE. Well well well –

GERALD. Whole family's on the skids, you know –

(**MARIE** *starts off:*)

WALLACE. Marie – !

MARIE. I'm just going to say hello –

WALLACE. No you ain't.

MARIE. As if I shouldn'ta known.

(to **GERALD***)*

Come on, you – You ain't gettin' in on the act.

(to **WALLACE***)*

I don't think this is right. Not one bit right.

(to **GERALD***:)*

Well, are you comin' or what?

GERALD. I'll be right out –

MARIE. No sir. You come now. I am counting to ten!

GERALD. I said I'm coming.

(Exit **MARIE***.)*

(looking out:) Not much for tits.

WALLACE. Yeah, but lookie those legs. And I'm gonna bust' em like a wishbone.

GERALD. Give you a dime if I can watch.

CORNELIA. *(off)* George – ? Sweetie?

GERALD. *(mincing, punching* **WALLACE**'s arm*)* "Sweetie."

WALLACE. Go home, now – And have the troopers send round a car in half hour so's I can pack her back to her mama's when I'm done.

*(*WALLACE *maneuvers* GERALD *toward a back exit; neither notice* CORNELIA *enter.)*

GERALD. I'm gonna stay and watch the show. Maybe take a picture. Hell, what I hear, she could use the dime, first husband threw her out on her ass, divorced n' hit rock bottom –

(They suddenly notice her. A beat.)

WALLACE. Uh – , this is my brother Gerald. He's just leavin. He keeps me company from time to time.

CORNELIA. *(formal and chilly:)* Pleasure to meet you.

GERALD. We met before.

CORNELIA. Oh? I'm sure I don't recall.

GERALD. Oh yes you do –

WALLACE. Beat it. Come on, Sweetie, I'll give you the grand tour. Start upstairs and work our way down.

(As they pass GERALD, CORNELIA *fingers his tie:)*

CORNELIA. Oh look. What an angry little grease spot on your tie. Better tend to that right quick, Gerald. Once a little grease spot sets, you just might be stuck with it for life.

(They eye one another, then exit GERALD. *As* CORNELIA *and* WALLACE *proceed upstairs:)*

WALLACE. It's a nice old house. I aint got no thousand dollar chairs or no sheets named Vera, but I do like livin here. Course, it's really the people's house –

CORNELIA. *(chilly; still stung)* Is it?

(They reach a bedroom: a brass bed, a large window, a table with some scrapbooks, a door to a bathroom.)

CORNELIA. Oh! How exciting – A mahogany bed! I do love a mahogany bed. The grain is so very masculine, don't you think?

(crossing to the bed)

An impressive addition. Does it have a provenance?

WALLACE. A what?

CORNELIA. A documented history?

WALLACE. Yeah, well, got a receipt from Ethan Allen –

(filling a glass from a pitcher:)

Care for some water? Don't keep no liquor in the house.

CORNELIA. *(crossing to window)* Oh! I'd forgotten – what a breathtaking view of the capitol.

(She lingers at the window:)

WALLACE. Cornelia – ?

CORNELIA. *(after a pause, from a soft place:)* Do you know who picked out this house? I did. One day Uncle Jimmy took me for a walk – I was not more than this high –

(indicates about three feet with her hand)

– and we passed by. It used to be Miz Lignon's house. Well, I said it'd make a much nicer Governor's Mansion than that ol' thing the State had us livin' in. So Jimmy bought it. I used to play in here. Mama and Daddy had this room. They had the bed over there –

(points)

I used to hide under it and wait for someone to find me. This is a real funny feelin –

(beat; from a soft and distant place)

Ever been back in the house you grew up in?

WALLACE. Oh, we had a few.

CORNELIA. No. There's just one. A particular place that lingers on. Speaks in your dreams at night.

(She sits on the bed, feeling the moment. He sits beside her.)

WALLACE. *(leans in close:)* Whispers in your ear, does it? Feel its breath on your neck?

(She deliberately splashes some of **WALLACE** *'s water onto her skirt:)*

CORNELIA. Oh! Gee-hova-to-gee-who! Look what I did. Thank goodness it's only water. Lend me your hand-kerchief for a jiff?

WALLACE. It's right here –

(He indicates his thigh pocket, inviting her to reach her hand inside. She smiles, does so, then dabs the water from her skirt. She hikes the skirt and flaps it provocatively to dry)

CORNELIA. If you promise not to tell a soul, I'll tell you a little secret: the air feels good. My legs get so hot. That's why I never wear pant suits. I prefer skirts – they're more feminine and I do like to show a little knee, but I get so hot. And those little skirts? The ones that only come up to about here –

(She raises her hemline to upper-thigh)

I cannot wear them, I just cannot. They're so tight and constricting, in here –

(rubbing her upper thighs)

It's a real paradox – you'd think they'd be cool, on account of being so skimpy, but they're not. They are very poorly ventilated.

(He's aroused. Having had her intended effect, she pulls her skirt down and briskly stands:)

There. Done.

(He reaches out and strokes her arm. She notices scrap-books on a nightstand:)

Oh my – are these scrapbooks? They are, they are – Look –

(examining a photo)

CORNELIA. *(cont.)* Ohhhh – You look not more than five or six. What is it you're selling?

WALLACE. Same thing you are.

CORNELIA. Pardon?

WALLACE. Pecans. Nickel a sack.

(He sits on the bed.)

Come sit by me and I'll tell you all about it.

(She flips a page:)

This here? I was 17. I sold magazines and encyclopedias. That white haired lady? She was a little blind lady up in Tennessee and I sold her three subscriptions. How's that for sump'n?

CORNELIA. Aren't you a slyboots.

(flips a page, then gasps:)

Oh, you are mighty handsome in that uniform, Mister.

WALLACE. Air Force. That's my plane, the Little Yutz –

(She guffaws.)

Bombin' raids over Japan.

CORNELIA. *(flips more pages; then setting him up:)* Will you look at this. These old suits – aren't you precious. What kind of fabric is that – it's all sheeny, like a little black wood tick. Oh, and those bittie little lapels – just like the ones Uncle Jimmy wore in the '54 elections. When was this taken?

WALLACE. Last year.

CORNELIA. Yes. Well, you do fill it out nicely –

(stroking his chest)

In here –

(and his shoulders)

And in this area –

(He places his hand on her leg:)

Tell me: how do you endure people's contempt?

WALLACE. I look like I care?

(*mincing, ridiculing:*)

"You got no business runnin' for governor, George Wallace, winnin' landslide after landslide – you not genteel enough." "Don't you go standin' in that schoolhouse door and upsettin' folks, George Wallace! And don't you dare be goin' up to Harvard and givin' the best speech anyone's ever given – "

CORNELIA. (*patting his thigh:*) Still, it's a pity how established, wealthy people of station do close ranks against outsiders. And campaigns do run on money. I'll tell you another supremely interestin' story. Hughlene Pucket is an old, old chum from Rollins College. Well, she and her husband Dale – you know 'em?

WALLACE. (*placing his hand over hers on his thigh:*) Nope.

CORNELIA. (*moves from under his touch*) I am agog. Speechlessly agog. They are practically the kingmakers of Florida politics. They give zillions – They are extremely important citrus people. I'll make a note to arrange an introduction. At any rate, in '68 Humphrey was virtually on his knees pleadin' for a handout – he was so indebted the networks cut off his credit the critical week before the election. You were havin' money-problems that final stretch, too, were you not? Well, anyway, Dale was considering writing a check for a grand quantity of money. Humphrey was waiting in the drawing room. And Hughlene noticed – his collar?

(*touches* **WALLACE**'s *collar*)

Right here? Tatty. And threadbare. Just like yours. And I noticed – are you ready? – these buttons, right behind his tie –

(*She unbuttons the top two buttons on* **WALLACE**'s *shirt.*)

These were undone. Gaping. And so – No check. Now, I'm the first to admit it's just a silly image thing – but it's so important to send the right message. I could show you how. If you like.

WALLACE. *(unbuttoning his shirt:)* You sure know a lot about politics.

CORNELIA. I ought to. Mama carried me to term stumpin' for Uncle Jimmy.

(He removes his shirt; she backs up.)

They – they say it's going to rain.

WALLACE. *(pursuing)* Yeah?

CORNELIA. That's what the paper said.

WALLACE. Good. We could use the wet.

CORNELIA. Have you found it a big hindrance being short? It's hard for a short man to become President. I believe Harry Truman was the last little fella to do it.

(He corners her and undoes the top button on her blouse:)

WALLACE. Aren't you a chatty little almanac. Gimme the Senators from Maine.

CORNELIA. Margaret Chase Smith and Edmund Muskie.

WALLACE. *(undoing the second button)* Gimme New York.

CORNELIA. Senator Goddell and –

WALLACE. *(nibbling her ear)* The Jew.

CORNELIA. *(trying to move away)* Javits.

WALLACE. *(pinning her)* Good girl.

(working on the third button)

Massachusetts.

CORNELIA. *(attempting to extricate herself:)* There's certainly the Saltonstall family – and the Cabot Lodges –

WALLACE. *(walking her to the bed)* The Senators –

CORNELIA. Kennedy.

WALLACE. *(pushing her back:)* And the nigguh?

CORNELIA. The what?

WALLACE. The big nigguh Senator.

(She frees herself and stands:)

CORNELIA. The Honorable Senator's name is Ed Brooke. Perhaps you should show me what you've done with the more public rooms in the Mansion.

(She walks toward the hallway.)

WALLACE. *(erupts:)* You stop right there – ! Let go a that door – ! Turn around – Who do you think you're messin' with? You think you playin' with one of your "nice boys" who sit out at the Country Club and drink ice tea with their little fingers stuck up in the air? That what you think? I ain't one of your nice boys and I've had enough of your silly games. Penny ante's over. Come on back over here. I have not had the opportunity to show you my political philosophy –

(He grabs his crotch.)

CORNELIA. *(laughs, superiorly:)* Ho, Governor, I am not interested in your political philosophy.

WALLACE. See, I got me the idea you are.

(approaching her, stalking and circling:)

I can get you excited. I get folks stompin' and cheerin' and goin' temporarily insane. I generate heat.

(puts her hand on his crotch)

You feel that heat? When I talk about hippies and beatniks and sissy intellectual morons – John Kennedy weren't nothin' but a big e-lite madam I put it to. And Bobby was his skinny little sister – she took it too. The Supreme Court – big, fat powdered matrons what never had it before. I give 'em pokes.

CORNELIA. You are vulgar and coarse.

WALLACE. Yeah. I am vulgar. And coarse.

CORNELIA. *(after a pause:)* What do you want?

WALLACE. *(pause)* What do you want?

(long pause)

WALLACE. Take off your stockings.

(long pause)

CORNELIA. Take off your pants.

(They break into wide grains then raucous laughter as they jump from their clothes.)

(Crossfade to **RUBY** *in her kitchen, a cigarette dangling from her mouth, wearing a loud floral bathrobe. She's on the phone as she fries bacon, laying it on paper towels…)*

RUBY. Cornelia's the same. The exact same. They been seeing each other for four weeks now, and I say, "Honey, slow down. You could have anybody. Think Nashville. Think Hollywood. You could have Warren Beatty."

(half-beat)

Warren Beatty.

(half-beat)

Doll, I gotta go, I can't think straight, it's just too early.

(As **RUBY** *hangs up,* **CORNELIA** *now in a bathrobe, stretches and yawns:)*

CORNELIA. Mmmmm – sausage.

RUBY. 'Morning. When did you get in?

CORNELIA. A little after three. When did you get in?

RUBY. A little after 4.

CORNELIA. Mama, your ashes are fallin' into the bacon.

RUBY. I have no minor vices.

CORNELIA. Must you wear 'em like a badge – ?

(She inspects a skillet on the stove:)

Bacon, too?

RUBY. Mmmmm. And hamburger patties.

(sensing **CORNELIA***'s disapproval:)*

I just felt like frying.

*(**CORNELIA** opens a window and stretches, breathing deeply:)*

CORNELIA. Mmmmm –

(yawns)

– still a trace of cool out…

*(**RUBY** plunks down a glass of O.J.)*

CORNELIA. Thanks. Guess who's just about to pop the question.

RUBY. Says who?

CORNELIA. He went to Silverman's yesterday to price a ring. I got spies out the wazoo. A Wallace and a Folsom. George and Cornelia. Anthony and Cleopatra. It's so, so right. We are both supremely public creatures. We both photograph well.

RUBY. I've heard it said there are deeper reasons for matrimony.

CORNELIA. Don't think I haven't been laying in bed all morning thinking about that. I like sex, Mama. I'm just realizin' that. I've always liked flirtin' – but I like sex, too. I like it a lot.

RUBY. *(growling, disgusted:)* I do, too, but it's 10:30 in the morning.

CORNELIA. You ever look at his hands? Thick. The hands of a prize fighter. He holds a fork – like a pitchfork, jabbing at the chopped steak – mmmmmmm. Gives me goose flesh. He's very strong. And a little mean. In a nice way. Not ugly mean. I mean just the kind of mean I like. All I know, I could stay in bed with him behind those green velvet curtains a zillion years. 'Til all the stars and satellites fall from heaven. When we're in that room – Oh God, Mama! – George, naked, dark skin and chest hairs and thick paws bending over me, draped on top of me –

RUBY. I've heard all I need to hear.

CORNELIA. Each time it feels like a million billion years when we're together. Like all eternity, from Adam and Eve straight through to the Second Coming –

(giggles, then sets up her mother:)

And when I look at my watch? I can barely believe it only took four minutes.

RUBY. Cornelia!

CORNELIA. When we were together last night – "together" – I couldn't tell if I was dreaming or not. I couldn't tell what was me and what was him. A complete unity of souls. He's huffin' and puffin' away, his eyes spinnin' and dialatin' – it's very spiritual and religious. Know what else? He yanks my hair. He takes a handful and he yanks me to the left, then he yanks me to the right, and I'm squeelin' with delight – What do you think about that?

(RUBY *braces herself, then pulls over a chopping block and a knife and briskly chops okra.*)

RUBY. *(evenly)* I'm happy you're havin' a little fun. Nothin' wrong with a little fun –

(tosses the knife aside:)

But marrying him?! The ink on your divorce papers isn't even dry. It's too soon. You can't go makin' decisions. You can't protect yourself.

CORNELIA. THE silliest thing I ever heard.

RUBY. I see. That's why your "ex" took up with that slut and broke your heart. All you got out of it was that damn red sports car. Least I always hold on to the house.

CORNELIA. I didn't want the dumb house and let's not start in on that again.

RUBY. I didn't bring it up.

CORNELIA. Yes you did – just now you did.

RUBY. Now you're gettin all defensive.

CORNELIA. I'm not defensive.

RUBY. Then why don't you wait a couple months? Ever think about that?

CORNELIA. No. And we're not gonna, either. Pass me a little butter.

RUBY. Sweetie, all I'm sayin' is George Wallace isn't exactly a saint. What do you really know about him?

CORNELIA. I know he adores me. And I don't need to know anything else.

RUBY. Honey, you got to dole it out. You got to hold back something. A farmer never puts down *all* the hay where the goats can get at it.

CORNELIA. I'm talkin' something so – stunning, and you're talkin "goats"?! Mama, I am awash in feelings there aren't even words for. When I'm with him in the Mansion, EVERYTHING just comes together – it's like the past and future become one. It's – breathtaking! Last night? I woke up and watched him sleeping beside me and I received a celestial message. Why I was layin' beside him – the very reason God put me on the dang planet. Mama, I can make George Wallace President! Goddamn, I can! I will! It's like all my life I been trainin' for somethin', and I never knew what it was til George. It's like Divine Providence – like I've been destined to be married to George – Like God made my marriage fall apart to free me for my earthly mission.

RUBY. Does it bother you George Wallace is a shit? A little race-baitin' shit?

CORNELIA. No. Might if it was true.

RUBY. There are some things even you cannot explain away.

CORNELIA. Don't be naïve. Politics is image. Image ain't reality. He doesn't believe that stuff, all those speeches. And that's my point – I'm gonna change all that, just you wait and see.

(**RUBY**'s not buying.)

For pity sake – He just took the positions the people wanted. If he didn't, then he'd be the dictator people say he is. It's just a perception problem.

RUBY. "Perception"?! You don't know – *I* was there. He was a little nuthin in the legislature til we took him under our wing and let him run the Southern Alabama campaign. George rode Jimmy's coattails to get his start. Oh, he was a regular little progressive, alright – til he hitched his wagon to another star when he discovered yellin' "Nigger" was a better way to get elected –

CORNELIA. Mother – !

RUBY. He doesn't even have the principles to be a racist – he's an opportunist pure and simple – He was like a son, a brother to us, then he stabbed us in the back to get the governorship and took it away from us. And now he's boxed himself into a corner with his race baitin' and he's grabbin' on to you and the family name as a meal ticket back to respectability –

CORNELIA. You're not being fair. Once upon a time you had a similar chance. Uncle Jimmy was elected – and YOU took it.

RUBY. That's a completely different matter – and don't you compare my James to that little cock-a-roach. My brother needed me. I got him elected. The state needed us – *We* stood up to the Klan – we abolished the poll tax – You were too young to understand. When I moved into the Governor's Mansion to be Jimmy's right hand man, I took you with me, AND I got your father a good job with the State.

CORNELIA. And didn't he feel so loved. Can't imagine why he left us.

RUBY. Don't you do this to me –

CORNELIA. To you? What about me? Oh, we had a fine time livin' in the Mansion, life of Riley – til everything crumbled, 'til Daddy walks off and leaves us, til you and me were O-U-T, livin' like homeless itinerant vaga-bonds from hand to mouth – drivin' old wrecks on the verge of repossession – One of your meats is burning.

(**RUBY** *burns her hand on the skillet and chucks it aside:*)

RUBY. Damn it to hell – !!

(pause)

CORNELIA. I thought you'd be happy to be back in the Governor's Mansion.

RUBY. Me – ?

CORNELIA. I thought you'd enjoy being the hostess again.

RUBY. Hostess?

CORNELIA. All the plans I had to remodel the guesthouse in back for you.

RUBY. You never said those things.

CORNELIA. Well, of course I did.

RUBY. No, you didn't. Hostess, huh?

(working it through:)

Well, I don't know. I can't just drop everything. But you do need someone to look after you –

(Long pause. RUBY sighs.)

Do you love him?

(CORNELIA nods. RUBY graons.)

CORNELIA. I can't help it. I do.

(long beat; awestruck:)

After all these years. Mama, we're finally goin' home.

(Crossfade to Mansion first floor. GERALD dials the phone:)

GERALD. *(into phone:)* Yeah – Gimme Seymore.

(beat, then keeping his voice low:)

Seymore? I know what you're up to. I know you're shoveling campaign money into bank vaults. I know you're stealing!

(beat)

Either you cut me in or I'll tell George and *I'll* take over the money cause I'll get George to say I can!

(WALLACE appears at the top of the stairs and runs down, buttoning his shirt, carrying a jacket.)

WALLACE. Man, you're so goddamn greedy. How come you so greedy?

GERALD. *(hanging up:)* I dunno. Just am. Listen, you made a decision on these – ?

(GERALD presents a stack of KuKlux Klan brochures to WALLACE.)

WALLACE. *(recoiling in revulsion:)* Woah – ! Jesus Christ no. Get rid of it. Hey, where the hell's Marie?

GERALD. *(yelling off:)* Marie – !!

WALLACE. Tell her to hurry up.

GERALD. *(calling off:)* Git in here!!

(to **WALLACE***:)*

George, I think you oughta okay these brochures.

WALLACE. And I said no. N-O.

GERALD. What's your rush?

WALLACE. Got a date.

(He slips into a loud lime green jacket.)

Whattya think of this little number? She says it's sassy. What the folks in New Yoke are wearin'.

GERALD. You look like you got Liberace's dry cleaning by mistake.

*(***GERALD*** shoves the Klan brochures under Wallace's nose:)*

I mean it – I really want the go on these –

(Phone rings; **GERALD** *snatches it:)*

Hello?

(peeved:)

No. No, no. He can't talk to you, we're in the middle of a campaign –

(exasperated:)

Aach! Jesus, No! Stop your pesterin' Cornelia – leave the poor man alone!

WALLACE. *(overlapping:)* Gimme that, gimme, gimme that phone –

*(***WALLACE*** snatches the receiver:)*

(moony as hell:) Highdy – Hi – Uh-huh –

(turns his back, then:)

Whatcha wearin, tell me what you're wearin –

(beat)

Whatcha got on underneath?

(**GERALD** *plunks the brochures in* **WALLACE**'s *lap:*)

WALLACE. *(cont.)* Call you back Sweetie –

    (hangs up, peeved:)

    Whaattt – ?!

    (**GERALD** *points to the brochures:*)

    NO!!! I don't want to start messin' with the Klan again.

GERALD. Why not?

WALLACE. Cause I say so, that's why. That shit's crass.

GERALD. Since when?

WALLACE. Since now. Since right now. And they're just real mean sons a bitches. Tell 'em thank you kindly, boys, but don't call us, we'll call you, and Jesus H. Christ where the hell's Marie?!

    (**MARIE** *enters.*)

    Hey, Marie –

    (hint of nerves:)

    Um, sit down.

    (takes a breath)

    Now, Marie – Gerald – I got a little somethin' I wanna tell you –

    (thinks again:)

    Well, you know –

    (beat; clears his throat:)

    There comes a time – In a man's life –

    (beat)

    Look, I'm gettin' married. That's it.

    (stunned silence.)

GERALD. This I don't believe. Can't you smell an opportunist?

WALLACE. Not since you been using that Old Spice Marie gave you. Marie, tell him not to piss me off.

MARIE. Tell him yourself.

GERALD. She's plastic and cheap! She's a fake! You don't see her when you leave the room. Holding court like some kinda royalty, then turns to me and says, "I need a drink." Like I was an errand boy. Hell, I don't even get my own wife a drink.

MARIE. And that proves exactly what – ?

GERALD. For your information, I been checking her out with our people –

WALLACE. And for your information, so have I –

GERALD. No one's gonna tell you diddley 'cept what you wanna hear. I get the truth – She's a divorced water skier from Cypress Gardens on the rebound! We're half hour late at Mobile cause we're waiting for her damn hair-dryer. Pain in the ass. At Huntsville, she tells me I ought to get advertising men involved in the campaign. She asks about finances, and why we don't buy a literature foldin' machine –

WALLACE. *(overlapping:)* So why don't we – ? Marie, get him with the program.

(MARIE sniffs:)

Great. Floor's all yours. What do *you* got against her?

MARIE. Against *her*? Not one little thing. And that's all I got to say.

(blurts it out:)

Maybe you're over Lurleen, maybe you're just all ready to move on –

WALLACE. Marie, I mourned –

MARIE. Not much. Not enough.

WALLACE. It's been two years –

MARIE. I don't care if it's been two-hundred. I still miss that little woman every day.

GERALD. Zip it, Punkin.

MARIE. No! Leave me be – I don't care –

(rising)

You think you can just empty her closet and drawers and go waltzin' off like she never happened. Well you can't. Life ain't that way. You aren't free to just erase the past – even if you want to – even if what you did was just – horrible!

(Exit **MARIE**. *Pause.)*

GERALD. You better start lookin' for a new campaign manager.

WALLACE. Oh then quit. Go ahead. Both you two are startin' to bore my ass off.

GERALD. I mean it. I swear it. I really will.

WALLACE. Ta ta.

GERALD. George, I get it. I do. Mama sewed our underwear on her Singer from gunny sacks. But now we're fartin' through silk. We're okay. You don't need her. She ain't like Lurleen. Sure Lurleen was a figurehead, but she was gracious and stayed in her place. This one's ambititous, she's after the limelight like every Folsom ever born – they're addicted to it, they get off on it. We swept them from office – good riddance to their liquor and their scandals. Ahh, but now one's determined to crawl back in. A little bug – little Cornelia bug –

WALLACE. *(erupting:)* You are a fool! A damn ignorant fool! Marryin' that girl's the smartest move I'm ever gonna make. For starters, she plays. Oh I've seen it, and that's what the folks *I* talk to tell *me*. She plays in New York and up North. Out West. California. She'll play right up to 1600 Pennsylvania Avenue –

(a beat; then from a softer place:)

And I'll tell you something else. I ain't never felt the way that woman makes me feel. Never. I know her fancy airs and Ohh La Las, but there's something beneath that, a fire, a spark – that gets me. Just gets me. Man, she knocks my breath away –

(beat)

WALLACE. *(cont.)* And I expect you to get along with her.

(half beat, sharply:)

I mean it.

(half beat)

Look at me –

(They hold a look.)

(GERALD *sighs in capitulation.)*

That's better.

(WALLACE *proceeds to leave. He pauses and regards the brochures:)*

Oh, fuck it. Use 'em if you think we need 'em. I don't give a shit.

(Crossfade to Ruby's Front Porch, ten days later. **COR-NELIA** *waits, anxious. She glances at her watch. Soon,* **WALLACE** *arrives.)*

CORNELIA. Hey there. Stranger.

(He smiles, but there's a distance between them.)

WALLACE. Hey, what's that music?

CORNELIA. That? I put us on a little Bossa Nova.

WALLACE. Yes sir, "Bossa Nova." You sure are sump'n. "Bossa Nova" – what's that stand for?

CORNELIA. Loooove.

(long beat; soft, moony:)

Jo'ge – ? What's on the plate for tomorrow?

WALLACE. Tomorrow? Tommorrow's Huntsville. Big rally at NASA.

CORNELIA. Mmmm.

(beat)

Honey? What about the day after?

WALLACE. *(a little chuckle:)* Ain't you heard, little girl? There's gonna be a vote.

CORNELIA. Ohhh.

(beat)

You gonna win, you know.

WALLACE. Think so?

(She nods.)

Really?

(She nods; he smiles.)

Me, too.

CORNELIA. Honey? What about the day after that?

WALLACE. *(He studies her:)* What's a matter, Sweetie?

(She shakes her head "no.")

Better tell me –

(She shakes her head "no.")

You tell me and I'll fix it. I'll have it killed, or sent to jail – I ain't without a little influence you know.

CORNELIA. Alright. I can read our stars. I can see the future. Clear as day sometimes. Come January – there you are, up on the inaugural platform, top hat, morning coat, takin' your oath, parades and big floats passing by. Thing is, what I don't see – what's become a little hazy last week or so – Am I still in that picture, too?

(He reaches into his pant pocket, produces a ring box and sets it down between them:)

WALLACE. I got me the idea you like me. Course, now, can't imagine why. I shore ain't no looker. Ain't got no money to speak of. And I am 20 years older. Don't know that I'd want me. So, guess I started wonderin' – maybe just a little bit – why it is you do.

CORNELIA. People been sayin' stuff?

WALLACE. Strong as I feel about you, I can't go further til I hear what you have to say.

(a long pause)

CORNELIA. I have always aspired to the loftiest heights – I say that unashamedly. So, if you're askin' – if I would marry you if you were just a – complete nobody?

(beat)

No. I would not. And you wanna know what else? You wouldn't marry me if I was the kind of woman who would.

(He chortles.)

When I was a little girl, I found a glowworm. And I asked my grandma Diddie what made it glow. And she said, "Babe, to tell you the truth, they just got the stuff in 'em." Well that's me, and that's you. And together? Don't you see? We're gonna light up the damn sky and just – shine.

(beat)

We are meant to be together, George, I know it in my bones. And I know this, too: God smites those who spit in the face of their god-given potential and just throw it all away. Destiny has put us together. And if I'm pushin' hard as I know how, it's cause sometimes destiny needs a helpin' hand.

WALLACE. So you gonna marry me or not?.

*(They kiss. **RUBY** enters, returning home. She observes their kiss, then crosses to join. She's been drinking. A lot.)*

RUBY. "I'm a mean dog, a keen dog,
a wild dog and lone –

CORNELIA. Oh Jesus, let's get outta here –

RUBY. A mad dog a bad dog
stealing silly sheep

WALLACE. Evening, Ruby –

RUBY. I love to sit and bay the moon
and keep fat souls from sleep!

CORNELIA. Lovely elocution, Mother, now do go inside.

RUBY. Oh I'll never be a lap dog,
    Cringing for my meat –"

CORNELIA. Mother – !

RUBY. What–?!

CORNELIA. You're not feelin well. Why don't you go on in to bed.

RUBY. *(growling)* I ain't tired and I feel just fine. What are you two up to?

WALLACE. Well, now, I just asked Cornelia to marry me.

RUBY. Well, well, well…

(plopping between **CORNELIA** *and* **WALLACE**; *ominously)*

Don't I love a weddin'.

CORNELIA. *(to* **WALLACE***:)* Mama's had a bit too much medicine –

WALLACE. *(off* **RUBY***'s breath:)* Whoa – ! What proof medicine you takin', Ruby?

RUBY. *(to* **CORNELIA***)* Why don't you go scoot on in to the house for a bit? Go on, skedaddle.

CORNELIA. Mama –

RUBY. *(reassuring sweetness)* Now, George and me are just gonna have a little chat.

CORNELIA. Go ahead. Don't mind me.

RUBY. Scoot. Scoot scoot.

WALLACE. I don't mind talkin' to your mama for a bit. I'll be fine.

CORNELIA. Give a hollar if you need me.

*(***CORNELIA*** exits to wait it out.)*

RUBY. What the hell do you think you're doin?

WALLACE. I am crazy for your daughter.

RUBY. That's SO sweet. That must be why you been callin' all over creation, callin' everyone to suss her out.

WALLACE. I have not.

RUBY. Tryin' to figure out what the effect will be, like you was pickin' a damn cabinet officer.

WALLACE. I've done no such thing –

RUBY. Oh stop wastin' a woman's time, I still got my sources –

(He laughs: big mistake:)

Oh you think this is funny, do ya? You cut the crap, George Wallace. I know you to the core and I'm tellin' you right now you hurt my little girl any more 'n she's already been hurt you'll have me to answer to, and so help me hannah I'll come down on you like a ton of bricks. I ain't afraid of you and you can't afford to have me against you 'n you better believe it.

WALLACE. Uh, Ruby, you ever heard a, "Sit down you're rockin' the boat"?

(She scoffs.)

You just a big sore loser –

(insufferably patronizing:)

– but it's alright, I forgive you.

*(**CORNELIA** quickly returns with three ice teas.)*

CORNELIA. Who'd like a nice iced tea?

*(handing a glass to **WALLACE**:)*

Darlin? Ice tea?

*(and a glass to **RUBY**:*

Mama?

RUBY. *(growling at **WALLACE**:)* What especially gets me is how you refuse to admit you were wrong. You'd just curl up and die before you'd admit to a mistake.

WALLACE. *(glib:)* Well, there's always room to be a little better person, I suppose.

RUBY. So tell it to the mommies and daddies a them four little girls killed in the church bombed in Birmingham.

WALLACE. Awe, shit, Ruby – !

CORNELIA. *(overlapping:)* Mama! That's enough!

WALLACE. Sayin that I'm responsible for that – That's asinine! You better lay off the sauce.

RUBY. Oh everyone knows you're responsible. You *are* responsible. For what happened in Selma at Edmund Pettis Bridge, for the whole sorry mess.

WALLACE. None of that happened, not one bit, not the way *you* say –

RUBY. People got killed!

WALLACE. You know, I'm just not going to talk to you about stuff back then –

RUBY. "Then"?!

(rustles in her bag for a brochure:)

"Then – "?

(Reads from the brochure:)

"Suppose your wife is driving home at eleven o'clock at night. She is stopped by a highway patrolman. He turns out to be black. Think about it. Elect George Corley Wallace – " Love your new literature, George –

WALLACE. We didn't send that –

RUBY. Oh they're all over town – !

WALLACE. I can't control every crackpot – !

CORNELIA. George just said he didn't know about that stuff –

RUBY. You know alright cause I know you know – !

(to **CORNELIA***)*

and I know YOU know –

CORNELIA. AND I DON'T CARE! JUST STOP IT!

RUBY. Other Governors came to power when you did, George. They were segregationists, too. We were all raised that way. But they rose to the occasion. They lead their states. You pandered. You bit Alabama on the jugular and filled it fulla poison.

(Exit RUBY. CORNELIA *holds the brochure, wincing at it. A pause.)*

WALLACE. What's a matter with her, anyway? Awe, Honey –

(half beat)

Don't be like that –

(beat)

Awe, Come on – look at me.

(She doesn't. A pause.)

Cornelia, lemme tell you something. When someone like me goes for the brass ring, well nobody's just gonna give it to you. That just ain't reality – Sheeeet. Sure, when I get out there speakin' to folks, sometimes I have to fuss at the colored a little, but I don't mean any of it. People let off steam with me. They get mad, like this New York cab driver who says to me, "these niggers been robbin' me blind and I'm gonna vote for you." Well, he goes into that booth and – yennnnnhh! he yanks that lever and he gets to feelin' better. That's better than if he went out and got himself all frustrated and hit somebody over the head. It's just politics, that's all. Honey, it don't mean a thing.

(A beat. She leans in, kisses him, then stands:)

CORNELIA. Two days later? We won a stunning come-from-behind victory at the polls.

(A shimmering spotlight slices down a few feet from CORNELIA *and* WALLACE. *She steps into it:)*

I insisted on a small, tasteful affair at Trinity Presbyterian –

(Enter RUBY, MARIE *and* GERALD. *An organ: "Here Comes the Bride.")*

MARIE. *(to* CORNELIA, *weeping:)* I wish you all the happiness that's in me.

CORNELIA. *(re* MARIE*'s tears:)* It was very emotional –

MARIE. *(to* GERALD, *sobbing:)* This was Lurleen's church.

CORNELIA. Intimate.

GERALD. (to **WALLACE**) She better stay out of my way.

RUBY. (overhearing **GERALD**) Shhh! This is a wedding, you turd.

(A ring on her finger, the kiss; Post Wedding Processional March.)

CORNELIA. And we're one, big happy family. United. Two dynasties. Now one.

(**CORNELIA** poses to the bursts of light from imaginary flashbulbs.)

And the new Mrs. –

(pop!)

George! –

(pop!)

C.! –

(pop!)

Wallace! –

(pop!)

Was introduced to Alabama –

(pop!)

The very next day –

(pop!)

On the cover of all the Sunday supplements and front page of all the Sunday papers – and above the fold! And for a honeymoon? It was off to the White House and the 1972 primaries. George and Cornelia, shooting the moon. And heavenly days, do we ever win!

(Music: "Hot Time in the Old Town Tonight"; "Hold That Tiger.")

Ballots rained down. Thousands. Millions. Gazillions. Like rice at a weddin'. In the North, in Massachusetts, they fluttered down like fat spring snowflakes – Little pieces of paper love with an "X" by Wallace.

GERALD. *(to* **WALLACE***)* Boston! We're stormin' the Citadel of Eastern liberalism!

CORNELIA. In Florida? Like orange blossoms in a gulf breeze, what *Time* Magazine called "a stunning plurality." In Pennsylvania? We gave 'em the biggest rebel scare since Gettysburg. In New Mexico, we weren't even on the ballot and we stormed the State like a gully washer – !

GERALD. *(to* **WALLACE***)* We're winnin' the Goddamn state in write-ins!

CORNELIA. By Wisconsin we have Humphrey on his knees! In North Carolina, they threw the Governor Terry Sanford at us as a favorite son. We knocked his campaign onto life support – then pulled the plug!

WALLACE. Not too bad for a country boy.

CORNELIA. Tennessee – Texas – Georgia! Oh, we are an exquisite team! And by the eve of the Maryland and Michigan primaries, we have over twice the popular vote of the nearest rival, and just as many more delegates. We are an unstoppable juggernaut surging on to the White House – !

(Family freezes in tableau. Spots on **CORNELIA***; symphonic version of Carpenters' "Top of the World…" *)*

Oh, and me? My 'lil contribution? I was everywhere.

(posing and mugging:)

Norman Mailer wrote that I was "certainly THE most glamorous woman in American politics since Jackie Kennedy."

(pop!)

Merv Griffin called me "George Wallace's secret weapon."

(pop!)

I'm the only one of the presidential candidates wives who owns a fur. And a white mink, at that!

---

*Please see Music Use Note on Page 3.

(pop!)

CORNELIA. *(cont.)* "Segregation" disappeared from his public utterances – he didn't say the "N" word once. Blacks were hired onto the State Militia. Oh, we were a one-two punch knockin' the political system of the U-nited States on its butt. It was a vindication of all I felt. It was all I knew it would be. I was utterly and completely triumphant.

*(***WALLACE*** *glares "Ahem"; she quickly corrects:)*

We were utterly and completely triumphant.

(Music trails off. Lights rise on mansion bedroom. ***WALLACE*** *struts in his boxers and T-shirt, dressing impatiently.)*

So. It's six in the morning, May 4, 1972, the day before the Michigan and Maryland primaries, pivotal states with a pot of delegates that are gonna put us over the top. George is skittish and nervous, so we're flying up to make one last blitz, takin' off from Danneley Field in –

(checks her wristwatch)

WALLACE. *(irked and impatient:)* CORNELIA!

CORNELIA. *(jumps, startled:)* Jimminy Crickets!! 20 minutes!?!

WALLACE. CORNELIA!!

(She dashes to the bedroom, laying out a green suit for ***WALLACE****:)*

CORNELIA. Darlin' – why didn't you tell me it was so late??

(pats his tummy to share the mirror:)

Slide over sex pot –

WALLACE. *(pulling on a shirt –)* When we get in a crowd, you gotta keep movin' – you constantly hold me back. You throw off my rhythm. I'm through the line and standin' there and there you are, way back over yonder, cluckin' with a bunch a hens – per usual.

CORNELIA. Sweetie, that "hen" just happened to be Governor Reagan's wife Nancy –

WALLACE. I don't care if it was Magilla the Hun –

(He reaches for an old black suit.)

CORNELIA. Honey, I set out your new textured green suit – it's eons nattier.

WALLACE. *(sidetracked, pomading his hair)* Just learn to work a crowd better –

CORNELIA. Don't use that gunk – I'll blow dry you on the plane. And I been workin' crowds since I was five, thank you very much. But if I may be so bold, I'd appreciate it if you'd introduce me to the dignitaries – I was mortified – off you went, plungin' into the crowd, leavin' me standin on the airplane – people lookin' up: "Who's the campaign bimbo – "

WALLACE. Seemed to me you were just too busy to interrupt. Laughin and yammerin' away in the press section of the plane – didn't hear my name once.

CORNELIA. For heaven's sake: they were writin' puff pieces about my favorite recipes. Lemme see your nose –

(He stands attentively while she trims his nose hair.)

I didn't tell you, one of Nixon's flunkeys said according to protocol the Governors would be received in the order by which their states were admitted to the Union – ears –

(He turns his head; She inspects for ear hairs)

I couldn't help but ask "which time." Stuffed shirt didn't even crack a smile. Why you suppose Republicans are so lacking in humor? There.

(He reaches for the black suit. She presents him with the Green:)

Honey, let's wear this one today. Textured suits are very "in." And green is very comforting. You don't want folks to laugh. These ancient black suits are scary. Even the moths won't touch 'em.

(The phone rings:)

WALLACE. *(punching the speaker phone)* Yeah?

MARIE'S VOICE. Is Cornelia there – ?

CORNELIA. Sure am, Doll –

MARIE'S VOICE. Billy Jo just called – Wants to know what arrangements need to be made for Thursday's lunch –

CORNELIA. Thanks, Hon. Tell him I'll speak to him at the airport –

(She clicks off.)

WALLACE. What lunch?

CORNELIA. I told you – I'm hosting the children from Partlow Home.

WALLACE. Won't look right bein' seen eatin' with an integrated group in the Governor's Mansion.

CORNELIA. *(applying make up:)* "Retarded Children"? On the contrary, Dear, it will *look* very right. I invited all the press – could you hand me that towel –

(He throws it at her:)

WALLACE. Stuff it in your mouth when you're done. And I said it won't look right.

CORNELIA. *(winking:)* Well, then, Darlin', *you* don't have to eat with us.

(into phone)

Marie, I was lookin' for Edward or Bonnie – I'm runnin a tad late – Could you find 'em and ask 'em to bring me my pumps? Thanks, Sweetie.

(No sooner does she hang up, another buzz on the phone.)

WALLACE. *(punching it on speaker phone)* Yeah?

MARIE'S VOICE. Cornelia, I forgot, your secretary just called and wants to know if she can confirm the Beverly Angelo Show –

CORNELIA. Yes, please –

WALLACE. *(yelling into the phone)* You tell 'em to forget about that show cause she's not ready and she's not goin' –

CORNELIA. Marie, just do as I said.

WALLACE. *(yelling over her shoulder to the phone)* Cancel it!

CORNELIA. *(hanging up:)* Oh, honestly.

(mock praying:)

Dear heavenly father. George is very edgy and nervous. The crowds yesterday in Kalamazoo were meanies and threw rocks and someone conked him over the head with a sign that said "God is Love" and hurt his feelings. Grant us serenity –

WALLACE. *(picking his crotch)* – and a fuckin' muzzle

CORNELIA. And Sweet Jesus? Please have George stop pickin' at his crotch in public. He won't listen to me. Amen.

WALLACE. You know, here on I think maybe you shouldn't be schedulin' your own advance. I think you'll be doin' it through my staff.

CORNELIA. If headquarters had a single good idea perhaps I would. Buncha good ol' boys. You're like the hen that layed the golden egg and they're the farmers standin' around too dumb to pick it up –

(GERALD stands in the door. An awkward moment.)

WALLACE. Yeah?

GERALD. Car's down front.

CORNELIA. *(coolly:)* Thank you Gerald.

WALLACE. I'll be right down. Cornelia's stayin' home today, so it's just me.

(Exit GERALD. CORNELIA grabs the phone)

CORNELIA. *(into the phone)* Bonnie – ? Pack up the hot rollers and the rest – I'm doin my hair on the plane.

(WALLACE ignores and reaches for his black suit:)

Sweetheart, please listen to me: clothes are a statement of who you are –

(lifting the two suits:)

I mean, there's no comparison:

(stroking and admiring the green suit:)

This suit is now. *This* is the man I married. *This* is the next president of the United States –

(He wads the green suit and throws it on the floor, grabs his old black suit and disappears, off. She fumes, dashes to her closet, storms through her dresses, jumps into an old Annie Okley satin cowgirl dress with "CORNELIA" chain stitched on the back. He returns in his old weevil suit:)

WALLACE. What the hell you doin'?

CORNELIA. *(zipping up the dress)* I'll wait for you down in the car.

WALLACE. You ain't goin' –

CORNELIA. And I am soooo sorry I made you late.

WALLACE. *(continuing)* – and you sure as hell ain't goin' in that hoo-rah.

CORNELIA. Darlin', it is perfectly plain I'm your little Cornelia Doll, to play with when you want, ignore when you want, pull a string and climb on top of when you want –

(tying a garish scarf around her neck:)

There. Ready.

WALLACE. Take it off.

CORNELIA. *(giggling:)* One step closer and I'm out the door and gone –

WALLACE. *(overlapping, stalking her:)* You ain't going like that.

CORNELIA. *(taunting as she backs away:)*

"Your gooo-ood girl's gonna go bad –

She's gonna be the swingingest swinger you ever had –

If you like 'em painted up! Powdered up!

Then you oughta be glad – "

WALLACE. I said change your clothes!

CORNELIA. Damn it, George, you change yours!

(half beat)

I mean it. I'm just doin' my job. You want me to be your Cornelia Doll, I'll be your good little Cornelia Doll. But you just can't go trompin' on my feelings. We're a team.

(**WALLACE** *chuckles.*)

CORNELIA. So – Okay?

(*He laughs.*)

CORNELIA. So – I'm goin?

WALLACE. Oh you bet –

(*Ugly; he shoves her:*)

So get goin'.

CORNELIA. (*still smiling*) Oh, stop –

WALLACE. (*shoves her again*) Move it. That's how you wanna go, then shit-howdy, that's how you gonna go. Get goin'!

(*He shoves her again.*)

CORNELIA. Stop it –

WALLACE. "Stop it"? Stop what? Huh?

(*He shoves her harder:*)

CORNELIA. I said stop it! It was a joke.

WALLACE. Yeah? Joke, huh? Big joke –

(*He grabs her arm:*)

CORNELIA. George, let me go. You'll hurt me –

WALLACE. (*twisting her arm*) Who's laughin'?

CORNELIA. I said take your stinkin' hands off me –

(*She yanks her arm free and begins to walk off. He rushes up behind her and shoves her to the floor:*)

WALLACE. Who's laughing now?!

CORNELIA. (*on the floor, frightened:*) What are you doing?!?

(*He drops down and straddles her:*)

WALLACE. Huh?! Who's laughin' –

CORNELIA. (*shrieking, trying to scramble away:*) I didn't mean it – It was a joke –

WALLACE. If you ever laugh –

(*He punches her.*)

CORNELIA. Owwwww!

WALLACE. ever ridicule – !

CORNELIA. *(hysterical:)* I'll take it off, I'll take it off –

WALLACE. Shut up!

   (He grabs her by the throat:)

CORNELIA. Pleeeease – !!!

   (He squeezes her throat, shaking her:)

WALLACE. SHUT UP!!

   *(**MARIE** appears in the door with **CORNELIA**'s shoes.)*

MARIE. George – !

WALLACE. Get out of here – !

MARIE. Stop it – ! George – !!

WALLACE. Get out!

MARIE. *(to **WALLACE**; assisting **CORNELIA** to her feet)* Are you
   out of your mind – !! Are you insane – ?!!

   *(**GERALD** enters:)*

WALLACE. Get your wife out of here – !

CORNELIA. It's not like it looks, I tripped – I tripped –

   (She lunges and careens downstage in front of the scrim.)

   *(A crash of cymbals! Spots slice down. Behind the scrim,
   WALLACE addresses a Rally:)*

WALLACE. *(bellowing, menacing:)* What good are so-called
   equal rights if it gets folks killed and ruins everything?!
   Huh – ?! First Nigger throw's a brick's a dead man –

CORNELIA. *(deeply shaken)* We flew out to Maryland 20 minutes later.

WALLACE. Give them federal judges barbed wire enemas –
   then burn the courthouse down! And the U.N.? Sheet,
   that's just a big cannibal club!

CORNELIA. We won both Michigan and Maryland.

   (devastated, fighting tears:)

   I ran into the bathroom and locked the door and was
   on my hands and knees prayin – beggin' the Lord for
   deliverance –

(A voice calls out: "Governor – ")

CORNELIA. *(cont.)* – for a sign.

*(The voice: "Governor – over here." **WALLACE** turns.)*

I honestly and truly believe that's why George was shot that afternoon –

*(A SHOT rips out! Four more bullets are pumped into him. As light fades on **WALLACE**, Life Magazine's cover photo of **CORNELIA** cradling **WALLACE** is projected on the scrim.)*

I ran forward and fell on top of him, instantly, instinctively, shielding his body with mine, protecting him from more bullets. And as the Secret Service grabbed at me, trying to pull me away, I came to know the truth in my soul: there is no way my heart would ever, ever let go...

(Fade to Black)

End of Act One

ACT TWO

(A spot on **CORNELIA**:*)*

CORNELIA. *(fragile:)* Where am I – ?

(confused)

What was I sayin' last?

(A spot slices through the darkness and finds **WALLACE** *sitting in his wheelchair in the Master Bedroom in his bathrobe. He's bored, listless, inert.)*

Oh. I remember now.

(beat; wryly:)

We did not win the presidency in 1972. Case you were curious.

(We hear unrelenting rain outside. Inside, a palpable sense of monotony.)

After months of surgeries and life support, the doctors released us from Maryland and we wended our way back. We touched down in Montgomery and multitudes crushed out onto the tarmac, greeting us with choking sobs and cheers and welcoming bands and genuine heartfelt love. Our people. George and Cornelia – were home.

(She picks up a box of papers and enters the bedroom.)

CORNELIA. Darlin. You're up. Sleep well?

WALLACE. Like the dead.

CORNELIA. That's nice. Glad to hear it.

(She proceeds to play the scene resolutely offhand, up beat, seemingly without a care in the world. She runs her fingers through his hair:)

CORNELIA. *(cont.)* Your eyes got a nice shine today. That spark of fire.

(indicating the box of papers:)

I had your secretary send your mail over from the office.

(She opens the curtains, gazing out:)

Still rainin'. Nice rain, though.

(returning to the box:)

I had her send over the mark-up of the Highway bill for you to take a look at.

(WALLACE closes the curtains.)

And heaps of get well cards and letters still pourin in.

(She notes the now closed curtains.)

The new Gallup numbers are out. Guess who's at 64% national approval?

(She casually proceeds to the window and opens the curtains again.)

Oh, why don't we keep 'em open for a bit? Kinda nice to let the light in. Shall I pick out a shirt?

(He holds up a hand:)

George – ?

WALLACE. Shhh.

(He intently listens to something. A beat.)

CORNELIA. What – ? Honey?

WALLACE. *(He listens, then sniffs the air, then shrugs)*. It's just – this is still all kinda new to me. I was just tryin' to figure out if I peed all over myself again or not.

CORNELIA. Oh bravo. Another gay-la performance.

WALLACE. Oh I'm just warmin' up.

(as she selects two shirts from his bureau:)

CORNELIA. Speaker Chilton came by earlier. Says we can pick up the Redlands district – I forget who's runnin' – if you make an appearance or send a signal.

(He ignores her; she lifts his head:)

Honey.

(reciting:)

"Amid the fell clutch of circumstance,

I have not winced nor cried aloud,

Amid the bludgeonings of chance,

my head is bloody but unbowed."

(half beat)

Here's a nice letter from Reverend Billy Graham.

WALLACE. *(utterly exasperated:)* Fuck him. Tell 'em to mind his own business.

(She laughs despite herself.)

CORNELIA. That's not funny.

(As she pulls out two shirts, He busily wheels to the window and yanks the curtains closed again.)

(She takes it in, strides to the window, opens the curtains, then presents the two shirts.)

Blue or green?

(Beat; he glares.)

Green. Now off with your robe.

(He turns and proceeds toward the curtains.)

Darlin – Cease!

(He pauses briefly:)

Now, don't mess with me on this. I'm bigger than both of us.

(He offers an "Oh? Is that so?" look, then defiantly proceeds to the curtains. She grabs his chair and pulls him away. He erupts:)

WALLACE. Stop! Stop – ! Let go a me!! Let go – ! Aaaghk! You just stop – stop wheelin' me around and dressin' me up like some damn rag doll you pull a string and says, "Ma-ma" "ma-ma" "ma-ma" *(His voice cracks:)* Ma-ma –

(pounds his fist:)

Ma-ma –

(throws his arms around her:)

Ma-ma –

(crying in her lap:)

Mama – Oh God – Mama, help me, help me...

CORNELIA. *(extremely uncomfortable)* George – George – Don't –

(trying to wriggle free)

George, please –

(She forcibly removes his arms from about her waist.)

(An awful beat. He composes himself.)

We are going to move beyond this. You're blessed with brains, talent – plenty a folks face stuff like this all the time. People's arms and legs cut off in lumber mills, or go blind weldin' or doin' whatever. They don't give up. You're a politician – you don't make your livin' with your legs. Look at FDR. He was crippled and elected president four times – you could do no less.

WALLACE. Who's gonna vote for the hate monger?

CORNELIA. Plenty a people! This is our chance to reach out to those blinded by hate to your message.

WALLACE. FDR didn't have television cameras when *he* was bein' hauled around like some half dead sack a potatoes.

CORNELIA. You could be the great healer. You could do for race what Nixon's done on China.

WALLACE. Does it occur to you I'm all washed up?

CORNELIA. Hardly.

WALLACE. Deader n' a doornail.

CORNELIA. Well if I believed that –

WALLACE. *(sharply)* You'd what?

CORNELIA. I'd just kiss you all to pieces –

(showers him with tiny, puckered smacks)

WALLACE. Uggk – uggk – stop – Cornelia, stop, stop –

CORNELIA. Then behave yourself. The eyes of history are upon you.

WALLACE. "History." History's havin' a fine time pickin' at the carcass of George Wallace. I know what everyone thinks – sayin' I got what I deserved.

CORNELIA. People forgive.

WALLACE. I hate forgiveness. Everyone looks at me fulla pity. I hate pity, too. Run on the Pity Party. The Pity Ticket. Governor George Wallace and 'ol Helen Keller.

CORNELIA. I doubt she'd run with you. She does not perceive of herself as an object of pity. Sides that, she's dead.

WALLACE. Perfect.

CORNELIA. You're hardly the first politician who's found 'emselves in a fix. Who's painted 'emselves in a corner –

WALLACE. Ohhh. So now you're on their side.

CORNELIA. Don't. Don't do this.

WALLACE. You think I did sumpn wrong.

CORNELIA. No sir. I'm not going down that road with you. And that's not what I said.

WALLACE. Oh yes you did. You think I got what I deserved, too. You think I brought it on myself. I know that's what you think. Well I don't care. I don't care. I don't care!

CORNELIA. Well it would seem to me you do.

WALLACE. Well I don't!

CORNELIA. *(bursting:)* Just – Stop!

(beat; difficulty catching her breath:)

George, politics, and a marriage, too, ain't so much different than professional water-skiing. The minute you stop going forward? You sink like a stone. You think about that.

(beat)

George – I am trying. I really am. Hard as I know how.

(beat; desperate:)

Fact is, I don't know much what else to do.

(He wheels closer. He takes her hand and holds it. A long, genuinely affectionate pause.)

WALLACE. Honey, don't give up on me.

(She takes his hand and brings it to her belly, moving it in circles up toward her breasts.)

Don't.

(She reaches down and unbuckles his belt, sliding it from its loops.)

(She falls to her knees and works on his zipper.)

Don't –

(beat)

Don't –

CORNELIA. Please.

(She moves her head toward his crotch.)

WALLACE. *(unable to bear it:)* DOOOOOOON'T!!

(He pushes her by her shoulders; she falls back onto the floor.)

(a dreadful silence.)

(She slowly rises.)

CORNELIA. *(composing herself; then:)* You must be hungry. I'll bring you up your tray.

*(Crossfade to Mansion kitchen. **MARIE** works in silence at an ironing board. **CORNELIA** enters, crosses to the back door and gazes out.)*

MARIE. Hello.

CORNELIA. Oh. Hi. I swear if it don't stop raining soon I'm about ready to lose my mind. When was the last time anyone came 'round for an interview? Ages, that's when – and don't think I don't know how shallow that sounds.

MARIE. How's George.

CORNELIA. Fine.

MARIE. *(after a beat)* I wonder what it is about pain and affliction that makes people think it automatically sweetens the soul. Some of the meanest people I know are cripples.

(They share a sweet moment.)

CORNELIA. Sugar, you don't have to do that. Go home. Staff can do it on Monday.

MARIE. Oh, I don't mind. I like to iron. I like the smell. There's cornbread in the oven that needs a few more minutes.

CORNELIA. You're so sweet. George is so grateful for all your thoughtfulness.

MARIE. Who says it's for George?

CORNELIA. Oh, Marie –

MARIE. It's what I know how to do to say – I'm sorry. For pre-judging you back when. I was so mad at what he done to Lurleen, and it blinded me. And that was wrong. And I hope someday you can forgive me.

CORNELIA. Oh sweetie.

(beat)

What'd he do to Lurleen – ?

MARIE. Puttin' her up to run for governor when she had her cancer. Driving her like a mule during the campaign, makin' her stay on in office while she was dying.

All she did her whole life was sacrifice to him and his political ambitions. Anyway, I'm just glad he's not in a position to abuse you – any longer.

CORNELIA. Oh. That. Well, that never happened. I mean, it did, but you just can't think about it. Like Scarlet O'hara – I mean, now let's face it, everything in the book happened to that one, but she went right on about her business – and she took over that lumber company and made a success out of it.

(beat)

She didn't much care for public life, did she? Lurleen, I mean.

MARIE. It completely terrified her! The crowds and public speakin. We used to go over her little speeches, practi-cin' in the mirror, lookin' up words in the dictionary. But the people were so good, they just took her into their hearts. We'd watch Lawrence Welk. And the Dean Martin Show –

(fighting tears)

She – she really liked Dean Martin's singing. He sang just the way she liked it.

(beat:)

She was so frightened at the end, doped up on mor-phine and just scared out of her wits. She weighed only 60 pounds, but he kept her on in office just past all decency. Poor thing was so embarrassed how she looked she asked him for a closed casket, but him – he slung her out in the Rotunda under a glass bubble for all the world to see! I know what he says, "Oh, I loved her, oh, I mourned – ," but that don't make it any better. Makes it the worse, to love someone and then go right ahead and just sell 'em right on down the river –

(an uncomfortable pause.)

CORNELIA. Well –

(CORNELIA turns and begins to prepare a tray of food for WALLACE. After a pause:)

CORNELIA. *(cont.)* Marie – what attracted you to Gerald?

MARIE. When – ?

CORNELIA. Well, originally. At the start.

MARIE. Gee.

(shrugs shoulders)

I don't know.

(shrugs)

Growin' up, we just had nuthin' to speak of. Oh, I don't mean we was worse off than anyone else. We never even really thought of ourselves as poor, everyone else was in the same boat. You just couldn't get a price for what you raised – cotton at eight cents. Well, my Daddy lost the farm when I was fourteen so I began working in Kress' behind the counter. Gerald came in one day, full of strut and swagger in his uniform – Seebees. We double dated a couple times with George and Lurleen – and she was workin' at a dime store in Tuscaloosa, too. She and I would laugh at how full of themselves they were. So cocky. I guess that attracted me. He came back on leave and I thought I'd never see him again. So I said yes, and that's how I became a married woman.

CORNELIA. Do you –

(lets it hang)

MARIE. Do I what?

CORNELIA. Nuthin.

MARIE. Oh, come on, Sugar. Whatever it is…

CORNELIA. Do you – do you still make love?

MARIE. With Gerald – ?!

(They share a laugh. A beat.)

MARIE. *(softly, with sorrow)* No, Sugar. Not for a while now.

CORNELIA. How do you – live with – that – loss?

MARIE. I don't know. It's just sorta something – it's just something you learn to live with.

(half beat)

Honey, sometimes things happen. Things change. Maybe life's not how you want it, or how you thought it would be, but – that's life and you just – accept it. Sometimes I think maybe about all you can do is just keep busy. You just gotta keep busy.

*(**CORNELIA** picks up a tray:)*

CORNELIA. Well. I'm gonna run this up.

*(Spot on **WALLACE** furtively dialing his phone. **COR-NELIA** proceeds toward him, then stops centerstage, overhearing:)*

WALLACE. *(into phone:)* Maida – ? You alone?

(beat)

What're you wearin? Come on, tell me what you're wearin –

(beat)

What color panties – ?

(beat)

Oh I'm man enough if you're woman enough –

(beat)

Tell me that you want me –

(A lascivious maon builds –)

*(**CORNELIA** claps her hands over her ears, dropping the tray with a crash!)*

*(Crossfade to Governor's Office: a massive desk, a chandelier, etc. **RUBY**'s alone, on the phone:)*

RUBY. I tell you true, Irene: Mike Wallace wants me on his network show in love and livin' color. Course, they don't want me talkin' to the press – But I say Hell with 'em, I'll darn well do what I please – he can't do much to Miz Ruby –

(CORNELIA enters:)

RUBY. Hold the line, doll –

(to CORNELIA)

Do you know how angry I am – ?

CORNELIA. At who?

RUBY. At that peckerwood you're married to! I asked him to name a building after Jimmy and do you know what he said?! He said he wouldn't name a shithouse after my brother! Then I got here and they said they won't let me in, they said, "You can't go in there, that's the Governor's office" and I said, "Do you know who I am?! My daughter asked me to meet her here!!," and you better believe they damn sure let me through –

CORNELIA. You been drinkin – ?

RUBY. Nuh-uh, not much – now spill: whatcha got cookin'?

CORNELIA. I got a secret. A top-secret state secret. A Fort Knox kinda secret that'll knock you on your fanny. But I can't tell you.

RUBY. Oh yes you can, oh yes you will – What?!

CORNELIA. *IF* I do –

RUBY. Of course I will, I promise, whatever!

CORNELIA. – you absolutely cannot leak. You gotta restrain yourself –

*(**RUBY** gasps! And lunges at the forgotten phone:)*

RUBY. Irene – gotta go!!

(She hangs up and resumes her attentive position.)

CORNELIA. Alright. You are familiar with the concept of Manifest Destiny – ?

*(**RUBY** nods vigorously.)*

And all roads leadin' to Rome? It's only been staring us in the face since day one. Remember when Uncle Jimmy let me put my initials on the underside of the desk? Well, this time, it's time to put them *on* the desk: "Cornelia Wallace – Governor."

RUBY. Whaaaat!

CORNELIA. *(bringing her voice lower)* How 'bout that? Didn't I tell ya –

RUBY. *(lowering her voice:)* I could burst! Why we whisperin?

CORNELIA. I told you. It's secret. No announcements – we're holdin' it close to the vest. We been talkin' about it for a while now. I was a little standoffish at first, but finally, last night, I decided Shoot! What the heck – he made his first wife governor and everyone came to love her. Think I'll make a good governor?

RUBY. Oh Honey, it's a breeze. Just be honest. Bein' honest is 99 percent of bein' a good governor. And no drinkin' or loan sharks –

CORNELIA. I sense there's a lot of affection for me among the little people, janitors, hairdressers and the like.

RUBY. Everyone's been waitin' for the next Folsom to come along. I thought it'd be one of your cousins – but I like it better it's you.

CORNELIA. Mama, I'm gonna be the best governor this state's ever had. I have so many ideas and I been reading a lot of books on the subject – about Napoleon and those Renaissance people in Italy. I got some impressive out-of-state support lined up. I won't say who, not yet, but let's just say some big money folks at Kentucky Fried Chicken have been takin' a good, long look at me – and with your help we'll turn Alabama into a showplace –

RUBY. About time, too. They still say this poor ol' state's saggin' at the bottom of all the national lists –

(but of much more interest:)

First thing we do is fix up the Ruby Highway. That'd mean a lot to me. It's in awful shape.

CORNELIA. You want it black-topped? You got it black-topped.

RUBY. I don't care so much about blacktopping – I want more signs up tellin' folks who it belongs to.

CORNELIA. *(a bit dreamy:)* George and me, we'll lay in bed at night, talkin' over the affairs of state. I'll say, "Oooouh, what about this, what about that," and you can bet he'll get a little cross with me, about policies and what not, but it's like that song "anything you can do I can do better," only not better, per se, just different, in my own way, and he'll see I was right – even if he can't quite admit it.

RUBY. You gonna use George's organization?

CORNELIA. Please. Gerald and all those yes-men urinatin' in the azaleas? No, Maam. It's time for outside professionals and heavyweights. And I want you to put the old Folsom machine back together.

RUBY. Darlin', I *was* the old Folsom Machine. *I* held the ladder while Jimmy hung the moon – and I'll do the same for you – And I don't drink near as much as you think I do. And when I do I take it on the front porch, not in the closet – I ain't a hypocrite –

(almost bellowing:)

I have never been a hypocrite!

CORNELIA. Shush!!

RUBY. *(as she grabs up the phone:)* Maybe in the past I mighta had one too many and gone showin' mah fanny, but I'm right as rain now –

CORNELIA. What are you doin – ?

RUBY. Callin' Grover at that rag of a newspaper to print up somethin' in the Goat Hill column –

CORNELIA. *(huge over-reaction:)* NO – !!

(She pushes down the cradle buttons:)

You're not listenin: you are not to breath a word of this to anyone –

RUBY. Oh.

CORNELIA. – least not yet. First we need to lay the groundwork. I need to brush off my image and get the real me out there. I've accepted piles of invitations for appearances. I accepted an invitation to appear on the Democratic National Telethon. And I'm gonna be a delegate to the National Platform Hearings in Washington next week. And I got an engagement in New York –

(**RUBY** *grabs the phone again:*)

CORNELIA. *(cont.)* Now whattaya doin?

RUBY. Callin' George. Least I'll congratulate the little linthead on his successor –

CORNELIA. *(grabbing* **RUBY***:)* Oh God, No – !! Least of all George.

(half beat, then a nervous giggle:)

Jesus, if George knew about this he'd probably skin me alive.

RUBY. George don't know – ?

CORNELIA. No. Not yet.

RUBY. But you said he knew –

CORNELIA. No I didn't.

RUBY. You said "we" – ?

CORNELIA. *(hesitantly)* Marian, my beautician – she and I –

RUBY. *(incredulous:)* Your beautician – ?! You cooked this up with your beautician?!

CORNELIA. Well – other people, too –

RUBY. Are you out of your cotton pickin' mind – ?!

CORNELIA. I don't believe he cares for the office any more.

RUBY. Well, he will if you do.

CORNELIA. He'll come around –

RUBY. Yeah, he'll kill you is what he'll do!

CORNELIA. No he won't, and if you're gonna be full of negativity, I really don't need to hear it –

RUBY. You're playin' with fire! You're out of your league! He'll kill you!

CORNELIA. Stop sayin' that –

RUBY. He'll take out a contract on you!

CORNELIA. Sit still –

RUBY. But he will! He will! He will!

CORNELIA. Keep your voice down and stop runnin' around like some chicken with its head cut off!

RUBY. He'll annihilate you! For God's sake, you're married to George Wallace!!

CORNELIA. *(blurts it out:)* You think I can forget that a single stinkin' second?!

(beat)

I didn't mean that. Not like it sounded.

(The phone rings; RUBY answers:)

RUBY. Hello? Hello, Margaret Louise – Doll, I really can't talk now –

(a beat)

Who – ?

(a beat, then chortles:)

No – She didn't – !

(beat, then gasps:)

She did – ?!

(beat:)

And wha'd I say – ?

(erupts with laughter:)

I didn't!!

CORNELIA. Mother – !!

RUBY. Listen here, Doll – Can't talk now – No, no, no, no, I can't talk – Cornelia's fixin' to run – I can't, I just can't talk!

(RUBY hangs up. A long beat.)

CORNELIA. No one's going to annihilate me. I've taken a certain precaution. I put wiretaps on his phones.

RUBY. *(beat)* Say that again – ?

CORNELIA. Bugs. Listening devices. On his phones and in the mansion.

RUBY. Does anyone know – ?

CORNELIA. No.

RUBY. Are you sure?

CORNELIA. I'm sure.

> (**RUBY** *stares at* **CORNELIA**. *Long pause.*)

RUBY. *(confused, bewildered)* I'll help you, Honey. Course I will.

> *(Blackout)*

> *(Lights rise on Mansion first floor.* **WALLACE** *seated in his wheelchair as* **GERALD** *descends the stairs, carrying a stack of magazines and newspapers.)*

GERALD. *(perfunctorily:)* Heya, George.

> (**GERALD** *sets the articles on the table and begins clipping them then puts them in a pile.* **WALLACE** *offers a heaving sigh.* **GERALD** *glances over, then resumes his work. Another heaving sigh.)*

> *(without looking up:)* Tired?

> (**WALLACE** *waits for* **GERALD** *to delve deeper, then drums his fingers in frustration. Another sigh.)*

> You got something on your mind, there, George?

WALLACE. Nah.

GERALD. You want somethin'? Some soup or glass a water?

WALLACE. Nah. Just that –

> *(a little laugh:)*

> – some folks have started telling me to think about runnin' for president again. Course, I say I'm not up to it.

GERALD. *(nose in his clippings:)* Yeah. You know best. Can't do what you can't do.

WALLACE. Well, I can't.

GERALD. Them days are over.

WALLACE. Even ol' Cornelia , though, she points to the poll numbers. I try to tell her poll numbers don't mean a thing, but she keeps a pesterin'.

GERALD. Just don't listen to that crazy woman.

WALLACE. The fact is, folks a gotten a little tired a George Wallace. You know?

GERALD. Yeaaahhhh. Fat lady finally done sung.

(off WALLACE*'s look)*

Well, you know, like at the circus – like a dancin' bear – First time you see it, can't take your eyes off it – like that talkin' mouse on Ed Sullivan Show –

(punches WALLACE*'s shoulder)*

You know – from France. Pepe Le Rue – No, that's not right. What's the name of that little fucker – ? That little mousey?

WALLACE. *(exasperated:)* Who the hell cares.

GERALD. What are you gettin' sore about?

(A beat. GERALD *resumes clipping. A silent simmer from* WALLACE.*)*

WALLACE. Well, what do YOU hear from the folks?

GERALD. 'bout what – ?

(off WALLACE*'s SCOFF:)*

You – ?

(a shrug)

I dunno. Nuthin, really.

WALLACE. Whattaya mean "nuthin"?

GERALD. Nothin. Nothin's nothin. Everyone's talkin' about Cornelia, about her "grand tour" –

(indicates his pile of clipped articles:)

Lookie – that there's a picture of Cornelia in New York – on Broadway for a gala event –

*(*WALLACE *could care less.)*

Papers, magazines, TV even – full of it.

WALLACE. I hear people ARE talkin' about me. I got boxes of cards and letters upstairs. Big boxes.

GERALD. Jesus, look at this – Here she is in Philadelphia:

(reading from a clipping with delicious innuendo:)

Quote: "Cornelia Wallace stood in for her disabled husband and attended the social functions of the three day conference," blah, blah, blah, "The unescorted Mrs. Wallace was in great demand as a dancing partner at the state dinner – a 35 year-old vision of beauty in a green feathered gown, her figure as trim as when she was a professional water-skier – "

WALLACE. Oh screw you.

GERALD. No, quite the prize, pretty young wife of the black cat. Everyone pressing her tight, dancing around the floor. Oh look – Daytona 500 – she's been out racin' those cars again – and water-skiin' too – Hey, Newsweek run that Shana Alexander article: "She is no ordinary First Lady. She is beautiful, brainy, and certainly the best thing that could have happened to George Wallace. She brings a sorely needed touch of class to the Wallace effort –"

WALLACE. I said fuck you.

GERALD. Oh hey, they do mention you: "Wallace, too, is an original, full of odd quirks and winks, repulsively engaging, filled with an egocentricism that will prob- ably save him. Little men never quit."

*(glances at **WALLACE**, then:)*

You're really gettin' sore – ! Don't get sore –

WALLACE. I ain't sore! Why would I be sore?!

GERALD. Sorry. Don't get riled. Whatever.

WALLACE. No! Not "whatever"! You listen to me – I coulda been president last time, til that crazy sunnovabitch shoots the shit outta me! It was mine! Don't you forget it! My whole life, thirty years of manuevering, scurrying around, to the right, to the center, creatin' a political image nobody in this country ever thought of creatin' before! No one ever seen nothin the likes of what I created – Ever! At the pinnacle, at top of the goddamn dung heap – We was born in a house with no indoor plumbin' but I won 11 primaries in '72! Shit! I lived in a five dollar a week room and washed clothes in the bathtub and lived on half-rotten potatoes – but I carried Boston! Then BANG! BANG BANG BANG BANG BANG! Sayin' I got what I deserved – !

(Pounds his chair in frustration. Long beat)

WALLACE. *(cont.)* Folks love me. Nobody's forgot about me. They love me – waitin' hours just to touch me – holdin' up their babies for me to touch –

(He sweeps the Cornelia articles to the floor, then wads up the lap blanket and throws it. A beat.)

Well I'm runnin. For President. Again.

GERALD. *(after a beat)* Is this for real – ? George – ?

(Long beat; off WALLACE*'s look:)*

Well welcome back to the land of the livin'!

(after a beat)

If you're serious about this, though, I think it's time Cornelia was roped back in. Get her back with the program.

(Instant spot on CORNELIA *stage right with small tape recorder. She presses a re-wind button, then plays:)*

GERALD'S VOICE. I overtly told him to rein her in. Now he spits on the floor when he sees her on TV. Poco a poco, Seymour. Poco a poco.

(She presses "stop," "rewind," and plays again:)

Poco a poco, Seymour. Poco a poco.

(As she clicks the recorder off, she thinks about the tape, tapping her fingers, then)

(Blackout)

CORNELIA. Hello – ? Who-who? I'm back –

(lights rise on master bedroom.)

(**CORNELIA** *proceeds to the room with her bag.* **MARIE** *greets her:*)

MARIE. Welcome back sugar. Have a nice trip?

CORNELIA. Fabulous!

(claps her hands:)

Good things, Marie, good things. In South Carolina, Governor West and I talked and talked, about education, mostly. South Carolina's doin' some very progressive things in education, things I think we could learn by.

MARIE. That's nice.

CORNELIA. How's George?

MARIE. Fine.

CORNELIA. Where is he?

MARIE. At the office, I think. He started goin' in again this past week.

CORNELIA. Really? Huh. Didn't mention it on the phone. Sugar, could you give him a ring and let him know I'm home?

MARIE. You bet.

(**MARIE** *exits.* **CORNELIA** *unpacks a few items.* **GERALD** *appears in the door, observing her. She suddenly notices him with a start:*)

(Long beat. They observe each other.)

GERALD. Look who's back.

(She ignores him and resumes unpacking. he enters the room:)

Have a nice trip?

(half beat)

Hey, now, what's a matter? Was there a little "snafu"?

CORNELIA. You're just so pleased with yourself.

GERALD. Cornelia, I don't believe I know what you're talking about.

CORNELIA. Just now. There was no one to meet me at the airport. Seems someone canceled my car. Someone acting on the Governor's behalf. I wonder who.

(He smirks and shrugs.)

Everywhere else I'm admired and respected. I am. You're the only one I know who looks at me as a threat. I just don't see why we can't have a truce.

GERALD. You? A "threat"?

CORNELIA. I don't want to be.

GERALD. Well, don't worry about it cause you ain't.

CORNELIA. Oh, ya know – what are you doing here, anyway?

(WALLACE wheels into the room.)

Darlin. Hello. I thought you were at the office –

(She throws her arms around him and offers a lavish, territorial kiss:)

I missed you. I brought you a present from New York –

(She hands a small box to him.)

WALLACE. *(to GERALD)* Say, where's ol Ruby?

CORNELIA. Honey – ?

GERALD. Where is ol' Ruby-doodle – ?

WALLACE. I think we oughta have ol' Ruby-doodle join us –

GERALD. Well I'll go get her, George.

CORNELIA. Alright, what do you two clowns got going on?

GERALD. I'll be right back, George.

(GERALD exits.)

CORNELIA. You wanna tell me what that's all about – ?

(beat)

WALLACE. I got a little news. I'm runnin for President.

(half beat)

You hear me? I'm runnin for president.

CORNELIA. I hear fine, darlin. I'm just wonderin' why you say it like that.

(a beat)

CORNELIA. *(cont.) (off mounting nerves:)* Oh – I forgot to call in for my messages.

(to the phone and dialing)

Hey, go ahead – open your present – go on –

(He opens the box and pulls out a necktie.)

It's Countess Mara – see, that's the insignia –

(into phone:)

Hello – who is this? This is Mrs. Wallace. Please put me through to my secretary. No, I want to speak with Bonnie.

(hold, then hangs up:)

WALLACE. Sumpn wrong?

CORNELIA. Seems my secretary's been fired.

WALLACE. Really? I wonder why that might be.

CORNELIA. Why you playin' cat and mouse with me?

WALLACE. You look like sumpn's real wrong.

CORNELIA. No. What? I don't know – .

(beat)

Alright. Yes.

(winging it:)

I'm very sad. Martha told me she and John are splitting up.

WALLACE. *(wheeling closer:)* Funny, I'm sad too –

CORNELIA. *(overlapping:)* No – Please – Let me go first. They're getting a divorce.

WALLACE. Who?

CORNELIA. John and Martha. Mitchell? The President's former Attorney General? Our friends?

(He gets it:)

It just devastates me. She, cause she truly loves him. And him, because now he'll be left all alone. It upsets me the waste – that they couldn't keep things in perspective and talk out their misunderstandings calmly.

WALLACE. "Misunderstandings"?

CORNELIA. Without instantly assumin' the worst.

WALLACE. Now, that is a sorry situation indeed, cause she's gonna be left without a penny.

CORNELIA. That's not my point.

WALLACE. It's mine.

CORNELIA. Well, I don't think she cares about that.

WALLACE. She oughta – You look at me when I'm talkin' to you!!

(wheeling closer:)

Yessuh, I'm just talkin' about the principle of the thing. Like she just got a little carried away with herself. Little too big. And now – a dee-vorced woman. And this – it was her second marriage, was it not? Guess that makes her a two-time loser. And a woman without a man – awe, that's a bad thing. Unnatural. Like an unemployed whore.

CORNELIA. Such tender sentiments.

WALLACE. I'da thought she knew better. Like she kinda brought it on herself. Like any other wife with half a sense woulda got herself back in line.

CORNELIA. Not if it was killing her. Not if she felt unneeded. Not if it was fillin' her with enough sadness to choke on.

WALLACE. Yeah, well next time you talk to her – tell her she's got about two seconds to snap out of it – before he throws her out on her ass.

CORNELIA. If you talk to him –

WALLACE. That's enough –

CORNELIA. No – If you see him? Ask him if he – still loves her. She – sometimes, she's not so sure.

(beat, then an attempted mood shift:)

God, I don't even know what we're talkin' about –

WALLACE. I was talkin to a little birdy while you was gone. Know what birdy said? Said "Cornelia's got a notion to be governor." Tweet. Tweet.

CORNELIA. And you believed it?

WALLACE. Birdy said it was so.

CORNELIA. Birdy's name "Gerald"?

WALLACE. Maybe. Maybe not.

CORNELIA. Honey, if I listened to all the baseless rumors floatin' around this house of mirrors –

WALLACE. *(overlapping, and stern:)* So there's nothin' to it?

CORNELIA. Darlin –

WALLACE. Look me in the eye.

CORNELIA. *(She does:)* Nothing. Absolutely nothing.

(Long pause; she crosses to the window and gazes out:)

(with deep fragility and honesty:)

Sometimes – ? I'm layin' next to you at night. And I'm so angry and resentful. At you. Then I float up to the ceiling and look down and all I see's two people layin' back to back, both starin' off into the dark. And sometimes? When I'm out on the road? Oh God George, I'm so glad to get outta here. Sometimes I can't get outta here fast enough. But I get confused, cause even that first night, in some cold hotel room? I just wanna come home. I put pillows where you ought to be laying beside me. I don't shine alone –

(beat)

We used to sit out at night. When the whole world was just a big front porch. And laugh and dream how we'd take the world by storm. And we did. I just want the dream back. All I've ever wanted is the dream back – And –

(fighting tears)

– if you don't know that? If I don't show it, or if – sometimes I do stupid things? It's hard to show it without gettin' at the part that breaks my heart, too –

(He wheels over and takes her hand. Long pause as they search each other's eyes. A truly, deeply tender moment.)

(The door burst open. **GERALD** *enters with* **RUBY** *in tow.)*

RUBY. Let go – let me go – let me go you cock sucking weasel – !

(She yanks free, stumbling, then lurches for balance. She's visibly drunk.)

RUBY. *(suddenly sees* **CORNELIA***)* Honey. Hello. When'd you get home?

CORNELIA. Jesus, Mother – You're plastered –

RUBY. *(laughing:)* Not me said the piggy –

WALLACE. *(to* **GERALD***)* Take her back out.

GERALD. *(in disagreement:)* What're you talkin' about – ?!

RUBY. *(flops on the bed)* Hey, George, come slip into bed next to me. Betcha then we'd see him get up and walk!

CORNELIA. Mother! Get out of our bed!

WALLACE. *(to* **GERALD***)* Take her on outta here. Cornelia and me had a little chat and there's no problem. False alarm.

GERALD. *(in protest)* George –

RUBY. What the hell am I doin' here anyway?

CORNELIA. WHAT is goin on?

WALLACE. *(to* **GERALD***)* NOW!

*(***RUBY*** proceeds toward the door. As she's just about to leave, ***GERALD*** defies ***WALLACE*** and calls after:)*

GERALD. Hey Ruby –

(very "leading":)

Don't you worry. We didn't say nothin'.

*(***RUBY*** nods, takes another step, then quickly looks back at ***WALLACE:***)*

CORNELIA. "Say nothin" what?

(to **WALLACE***)*

What's he drivin' at?

RUBY. *(scuttling out:)* Uh – I'll come back later –

CORNELIA. *(grabbing* RUBY*'s arm:)* What have you gone and done – ?

RUBY. *(pure distraction:)* Wait – !

(bellowing:)

HANK WILLIAMS JUNIOR JUST FELL OFF A CLIFF IN ARKANSAS!!

CORNELIA. *(gets it; knowing)* No – You didn't –

RUBY. Now – whatever you're thinkin', it's not like that –

CORNELIA. Oh no –

RUBY. I just asked George a hypothetical question –

CORNELIA. "Hypothetical" – ?!

RUBY. I only said personally, hypothetically, *I'd* love to see you Governor –

(CORNELIA *gasps!*)

That's all I said –

(to WALLACE*:)*

You tell her that's all I said – !

GERALD. *(produces a newspaper)* Not quite.

CORNELIA. *(to* RUBY, *gasping:)* You went to the press – ?!

RUBY. Did I?

CORNELIA. George – No – this is outta context – I was only flirtin with the idea –

RUBY. "Flirtin" – ?!

CORNELIA. Just day dreamin' out loud –

RUBY. You never once said "flirtin" – You signed the papers!

CORNELIA. HUSH UP!

RUBY. *(overlapping)* But that's not right – How's I supposed to know you was just "flirtin – "?! And I told you it was a pretty poor idea in the first place – !

(GERALD *reads from the newspaper:*)

GERALD. Quote: "Ask anybody: George ain't had his mind on business in a long, long time. He stays in bed all day and cries in Cornelia's arms and calls her 'mama'."

RUBY. *(defiantly, to* **GERALD***)* I never said that, not like that – !

(to **WALLACE/CORNELIA***:)*

He's readin' it bad –

GERALD. "Ensconced in the gatehouse behind the mansion for the rambling interview on Cornelia's candidacy, Big Ruby shared her diminishing supply of bourbon with reporters, then called a liquor store and persuaded the manager to accept a $5.10 check "that's probably gonna bounce like the last one I gave you."

RUBY. *(proudly:)* Drunk or sober, I tell it like it is – !

*(***CORNELIA** *tries to grab the paper, but* **GERALD** *continues:)*

GERALD. "She then picked up a phone and called in a local radio talkshow and asked the listeners to call in and pray for Cornelia's drug addiction problem – "

*(***CORNELIA** *gasps!)*

"Cornelia is not known to have a drug addiction problem – "

RUBY. *(yelling at* **GERALD***)* Well of course she don't!!

(truly puzzled:)

Why would I have done that – ?

CORNELIA. How could you have done such a thing – ? How could you – ?

RUBY. *(like a good-girl:)* I should go be alone and just think about what I done –

*(***RUBY** *tries to scuttle out;* **CORNELIA** *grabs her arm:)*

CORNELIA. You were asked to restrain yourself –

RUBY. *(defiant)* Look, I tried to help 'n I got mixed up –

CORNELIA. To cease your reckless behavior – but you swing down on your vine doin' your Joan of the Ozarks routine –

RUBY. Stop! I can't think straight – !

CORNELIA. No – Fillin' up your hopeless addiction to be center of attention –

RUBY. I'm not "addicted" to nothin!!

> (*pointing at* **WALLACE**)

> This is HIS doin' – ! HE's turnin' you against me – ! He's out to get us – Not even a mama's love for her daughter is sacred –

CORNELIA. (*overlapping fury unleashed:*) no no No NO NO! NO!! NO!!! You're not draggin' me down with you – Not again!! I don't need you – I don't want you – I don't even want to lay eyes on you!! You're evil! Pack your bags and get out of my sight! Now! Leave! Get out! GET OUT GET OUT GET OUT!!!

> (**CORNELIA** *races off.* **RUBY**, *devastated and stunned, struggles for dignity and composure.*)

> (**GERALD** *holds up both hands – "I'm not responsible for this mess," – then exits. A long pause.*)

RUBY. (*utterly devastated:*) I'm not evil.

> (*confused:*)

> I don't understand. I love everybody. I do.

> (*Long pause. Ashamed, devastated,* **RUBY** *avoids* **WALLACE**'s *gaze:*)

> This was my bedroom. When I was married. Twenty years ago but – seems like yesterday. When Lloyd and I fought, Cornelia used to cry and hide under the bed. See, Lloyd didn't like it here. Problem is, I do. So he left us.

> (*long beat, near tears*)

> First time I walked into this room, I thought "Will ya take a look at me." But who tells you the price of things? I knew enough to know I'd have to fight like heck to hold on to it. No one was there to tell me it's really the other way around. From the minute you walk in – Jesus, you can't never get free.

> (*quickly collecting her things:*)

> Oh God I'm gettin' outta this place and this time I'm never comin' back, never, ever, ever –

WALLACE. I am so sorry, Ruby –

RUBY. No – ! Don't! Don't say another word – !

(**RUBY** *breaks into tears and flees.*)

(*Blackout*)

(*Introductory chords from a steel guitar, then…*)

(*Spot hits* **CORNELIA**, *standing center stage, holding a mic. She sings a song in the veign of "Stand By Your Man" by Tammy Wynette, a melody which wryly invokes Cornelia's loss and self-asseration.**)

(*Blackout on* **CORNELIA**. *Applause for* **CORNELIA**, *continues over:*)

(*Lights snap up on* **WALLACE** *and* **GERALD** *in the Green Room of a TV Talk Show.* **WALLACE** *is extremely agitated.*)

WALLACE. She ain't supposed to be singin! No one said nothin' about her singin!

GERALD. Keep your mind on your speech. Folks here in Tampa love you.

WALLACE. (*wheeling about in agitation:*) She's turnin' this into some celebrity night at the Opery – She's supposed to introduce me, not perform a one-woman hootnanny –

(*glances at his wristwatch*)

She's already taken up four minutes – we only got sixteen! SHE's NOT SUPPOSED TO SING! This is MY campaign – God, if I could get my leg out of this chair I'd kick her ass for pullin this crap –

GERALD. There's nothin wrong with my leg –

WALLACE. How do you suppose it is – I love the Folsoms. Always have. But they all the kind that turn on you, aren't they?

(*A rolling ripple of laughter from offstage:*)

WALLACE. Jesus – now it's the fuckin' Don Rickles hour or sumpn – I'm gonna crucify her for this –

** Please See Music Use Note on Page 3

GERALD. No you ain't.

WALLACE. Yes, I am!

GERALD. No. You ain't. You can't. You're over a barrel – you're in the middle of a campaign. You can't do a thing to her. Not in public. Especially the "new" George Wallace. The "niiiiiiiice" George Wallace.

(Another ripple of offstage laughter.)

WALLACE. What's she doing – ? What is so goddamn funny – ?!

(GERALD clicks the remote at a playback monitor in the room. We hear CORNELIA and a WOMAN INTERVIEWER piped in:)

INTERVIEWER. Mrs. Wallace –

CORNELIA. Cornelia.

INTERVIEWER. Cornelia, you have been quoted as saying, any man who seeks the highest office in the land is overcompensating for some inadequacy. What's your husband's inadequacy?

CORNELIA. Well, I think a lot of people, that um, achieve or are successful at whatever it is, probably don't feel like – they probably achieve more because they don't feel like they were pretty, if you were a girl –

INTERVIEWER. Well what is George Wallace's inadequacy that he's over compensating for?

CORNELIA. He's short.

(off audience's laughter:)

No – no – It's a rather established thing. You'll find it's a psychologically proven fact that short men, men under five ten, feel a little inadequate –

(GERALD clicks it off, turns to WALLACE.)

WALLACE. Why is she doing this to me?!

(WALLACE puts his head in his hands. Long beat.)

(He looks up at GERALD. Long beat.)

GERALD. This is your last chance. Win this one our way. Not their way. Not her way.

WALLACE. *(beat)* I'm still ahead? Still solid in the polls?

GERALD. Florida loves you. You're up by eight.

WALLACE. When we get to the airport to fly on to Orlando, Cornelia will return to Montgomery. Give her the opportunity to come to her goddamn senses.

(blackout)

(In blackout we hear sounds of a car chase: squealing tires, rapid acceleration, skidding, etc. Finally the car halts, the engine cuts, a door opens then quickly shuts.)

(Lights rise: **CORNELIA** *stands stage left,* **RUBY** *stands on her porch stage right in a chocolate brown gaucho outfit, complete with Bolero hat with dingle balls.)*

CORNELIA. I cut over two lanes on Adams, whipped through the alley to Perry and left 'em eatin' my dust. In a station wagon, no less. I'm startin' to get good at it.

RUBY. What are you doin?

CORNELIA. Hidin'.

RUBY. From who?

CORNELIA. Spies.

RUBY. *(This seems plausible.)* Oh.

(half beat)

What's goin on?

CORNELIA. Just got back from Florida two nights ago. Couple a days early.

(Pause. **RUBY**'s *wounded pride and hurt speaks volumes.)*

CORNELIA. You look nice.

RUBY. Your cousin Janelle said she saw you.

CORNELIA. No – I haven't seen Janelle.

RUBY. I said *she* saw *you.* She was comin' back from Eufala, two in the morning. You were in the station wagon in the alley, sleepin in the back, curled up in a nest a bumper-stickers.

CORNELIA. *(shrugs:)* They lock me out sometimes.

RUBY. You're not right

CORNELIA. I said awful things to you. I didn't mean it. I'm sorry.

(beat)

Think I could spend a few nights with you?

RUBY. Oh, honey.

*(**RUBY** embraces **CORNELIA** and leads her into the house.)*

Your old room's a mess. We'll put you on the fold out. I need to move my files and straighten up a bit.

*(**RUBY** proceeds to clear piles of crap off the fold-out sofa. **CORNELIA** paces, anxious, agitated, occasional nervous laughter.)*

CORNELIA. You would not believe all the stuff they're tryin' to do to me. They're tryin' to make me crack. They log my calls, open all my mail before I get it. They're turning the FBI on to me. Maybe the CIA. I've been banished from the campaign – which is in tatters, by the way. They even got someone at headquarters croppin' and airbrushin' me out of all the photographs. They're tryin' to keep me away from George is what they're doing. God – after two months of carefully crafted image portraying him as vital and vigorous – the fools drop him on the tarmac at the Pensacola Airport on National TV, he breaks his leg in three places and doesn't even know it for a week. Mama, my name's not on a single check for the entire six years we been married – not even beauty shoppe money. I've got nothing. I've maintained the "glamorous" image of first lady on what I could save on my grocery allowance. Maybe I could get a job promotin' Florida Orange Juice! Part time, course. Wouldn't that be an answer to my prayers.

*(**RUBY** turns, sofa cleaned:)*

RUBY. There. Now. Sit. Come sit. Now, tell me everything that's goin on. Tell me every last little bit.

CORNELIA. *(stunned and devastated:)* I just did.

RUBY. Oh. Well. Good. I sure am glad you come back hone. I missed you. Hey – I got me a new boyfriend. His name's Joe. It's only been two weeks, but who knows. He tells me what he does for a livin', but I can never seem to remember.

(off CORNELIA*'s stunned expression:)*

What's a matter?

CORNELIA. Oh Mama.

RUBY. Now, don't you worry. I know it's bad, whatever it is, but we'll get us a good lawyer 'n come down on them like a ton a bricks. We'll drag 'em by their peckers through every tabloid in the country 'n you better believe it.

(long pause)

Honey?

CORNELIA. I miss George.

RUBY. Oh.

(shrugs)

We're both that way. You 'n me. We're people people.

CORNELIA. Is that it?

RUBY. You bet.

CORNELIA. I just miss him so much.

RUBY. Everything's gonna be okay. You wanna wear my hat? Here –

*(*RUBY *removes the hat from her head and holds it out for* CORNELIA.*)*

(Blackout)

(Lights on Governor's Mansion. MARIE *vacuums the stairs, determined, intently humming "Happy Days Are Here Again," irony intended. After a long beat, from offstage,* GERALD *calls out:)*

GERALD. *(off)* George – George!

(As **MARIE** *finishes the song,* **WALLACE** *suddenly enters in his wheelchair, careening about erratically.* **GERALD** *enters soon after:)*

Florida's just one primary, George. No big deal.

WALLACE. Aach! I've had it – I'm too old for this shit. This thing's a stink bomb that's collapsing beneath me!

GERALD. You can't stop – how can you stop – what happens if you stop?

WALLACE. I'm sick of it. Why don't YOU run for president – your wife on one side of the country and you on the other and people throwin' bricks at you. You give me the names of all the women you see at all the bars here in town and I'll stay home!

GERALD. I gotta go to the can.

(He lopes from the room. **MARIE** *and* **WALLACE** *stare at one another.)*

WALLACE. Whatta you lookin at?

MARIE. Nothin.

WALLACE. Oh leave me alone.

MARIE. Part of me feels sorry for you. Almost.

WALLACE. Here we go. Yak yak yak yak yak yak yak yak.

MARIE. You said you wanted to do good deeds. You wanted to help folks. I believed in you. We all believed in you. "The Fightin' Little Judge." I'm sorry you're stuck in that chair, I'm so, so sorry, but far as I'm concerned you brought it on yourself, every last little bit.

WALLACE. And don't you think I ain't figured that out – ?!

MARIE. Then I am sorry for you. After all you done, what an awful thing it must be, to be stuck in that chair, and finally be saddled – with a conscience.

(As **MARIE** *and* **WALLACE** *glare at one another, the phone proceeds to ring.)*

*(**MARIE** exits. The phone continues.)*

GERALD. *(off)* Marie, you gettin' that?

(beat:)

PHONE – !

(GERALD *enters, tucking his shirt into his pants:)*

Cripes. Like I have to do everything 'round here.

(picks up the phone:)

Hello – ?

*(Spot on **CORNELIA** at **RUBY**'s, phone to her ear.)*

CORNELIA. This is the first lady. Please, I'd like to speak with my husband.

(GERALD *hangs up.* **CORNELIA** *redials.)*

WALLACE. Who's that?

GERALD. Nobody.

*(The phone rings. As **GERALD** snatches it up, the receiver dis-assembles in his hand; the mouth-piece cover falls to the floor. We hear a huge SCREEEEEEEEEEECH.)*

CORNELIA. Hello – ? Hello – ? George – ?

(GERALD *stoops to pick up the pieces.)*

CORNELIA. Please. Please put me through –

(Dial tone)

(GERALD *examines a small transistor-like device in his hand.)*

GERALD. *(to* **WALLACE***)* I don't suppose you went and put this little poodle on the phone?

(GERALD *and* **WALLACE** *exchange a knowing look.)*

WALLACE. Jesus. It's not possible.

(blackout)

(In blackout, we hear the sound of pouring rain.)

*(Lights rise. **MARIE**, center stage, stares into the darkness; **CORNELIA** stands in the wings.)*

MARIE. *(as though calling to a frightened animal)* Cornelia – ? Is that you – ?

CORNELIA. *(confused)* Marie – ?

MARIE. It's me, honey. What are you doing?

CORNELIA. Just thought I'd come say "hey."

MARIE. Honey, everyone's been lookin' for you for two days – Where you been?

CORNELIA. *(shrugs, then:)* Is George up?

MARIE. Sugar – Sugar, somethin's up – and whatever it is, it ain't good. State Patrol's been here – They been givin' lie detector tests to everyone – I think you better get outta here –

CORNELIA. No. I think everything's gonna be okay now.

MARIE. No, Sugar, it's not. Run. Run fast, some place far away from here –

CORNELIA. Oh Marie. Don't you know? There is no place else but here.

(GERALD enters.)

GERALD. There you are. How you been? We been lookin' high and low for you. Oh – Governor would like to have a word with you.

CORNELIA. *(hopeful)* He would?

(GERALD nods.)

Now?

GERALD. Right now.

CORNELIA. *(to MARIE)* See?

GERALD. *(to MARIE)* I think you best go home a bit.

(GERALD leads CORNELIA into the house.)

MARIE. Sugar – ?

(CORNELIA turns back; long beat:)

Good night.

(Lights up on bedroom as GERALD ushers CORNELIA in. WALLACE sits with his back turned, staring out the window. It's difficult for him to face her.)

CORNELIA. *(to* WALLACE*)* Darlin – ? Hello.

> *(kisses his cheek; a beat)*

You wanted to see me?

> *(after an awkward pause:)*

It's awful late. What – what are we doin'?

GERALD. It's been so awful hot. Can't sleep. Been hot, huh, George?

CORNELIA. It's cooled off with the rain. There's a breeze.

GERALD. Nuh uh. It's hot.

> *(to* WALLACE*)*

Hey, George, you thirsty?

> *(to* CORNELIA*)*

Maybe you could order up a jar of that special lemonade?

CORNELIA. Is there somethin' goin' on? Has something happened?

> *(tenderly)*

Honey – ? Have you been – cryin'?

GERALD. Just order up the lemonade.

CORNELIA. Well – certainly.

> *(She turns to exit.)*

GERALD. NO! Use the phone. Save time.

CORNELIA. I don't believe the staff's in this evening –

GERALD. Oh, sure they are. Just pick up the phone and call down.

CORNELIA. Alright.

> *(She picks up the phone and dials. The receiver disassembles in her hand. She pivots, trying to reassemble it. Panic sweeps her face.)*

GERALD. Something wrong?

CORNELIA. No, nothing. Uh – no one's in.

GERALD. *(moving closer:)* Let it ring a bit. Gotta give 'em a chance…

(**GERALD** *yanks the cord; the receiver falls to the floor.*
WALLACE *turns around to witness.* **GERALD** *picks up
the bug and presents it to* **CORNELIA**:)

GERALD. What you done is highly illegal. A federal offense.

CORNELIA. I don't know what you're talking about.

GERALD. Department of Public Investigation's got a file on
you this thick and you gonna go to jail.

CORNELIA. I – I do not care for your tone or your
insinuations – whatever they are –

(*to* **WALLACE**)

I – I don't even know what he's doing here –

GERALD. Oh get off it. You did it and you're lyin' through
your teeth –

CORNELIA. No! Did what – ?! George!? Someone please tell
me what's goin on?!

GERALD. (*He plunks down a cardboard box containing tapes:*)
They got all your bugs and copies of all your tapes and
you gonna rot in jail! They gonna throw the book at
you. You gonna be in every paper in the land – and
above the fold!

(**WALLACE** *holds the bugging device:*)

WALLACE. Did you do this?

CORNELIA. What?! No! God, I swear I don't even know
what anyone's talkin' about –

WALLACE. After all we been through, did you do this?

CORNELIA. NO! NO NO NO!!

GERALD. Then all these – taped conversations – who the
hell put 'em in YOUR wall safe? Marie?!! The Avon
Lady?!?

CORNELIA. No – You! For all I know – you're the one's the
common crook, the back-room Rasputin –

GERALD. And who the hell are you – ?!

CORNELIA. Get out! You get out – ! I want you to leave our
bedroom!

GERALD. You think you're sooo superior. Think you're such
a princess –

(He grabs her:)

CORNELIA. Get away – Don't touch me!

GERALD. You ain't no princess –

CORNELIA. I said let me go –

(He forces the bug into her hand:)

GERALD. Take it – take it – This is who you are – a lying common criminal – a Judas stabbin your husband!

(She spits! in his face.)

WALLACE. Please leave us be.

*(Exit **GERALD**.)*

CORNELIA. *(deeply frightened)* They said our marriage wouldn't last a year –

WALLACE. Do you know what you have done?

CORNELIA. *(cont.)* – then you were shot and they said I wouldn't stay a year –

WALLACE. You have thoroughly humiliated me.

CORNELIA. *(cont.)* – it's been seven years. I'm just tryin' to hold steady in the saddle.

WALLACE. You've pulled some real boners in your time, but this one – oh, even you must admit this one just takes the cake.

CORNELIA. I thought – if I could find out who was against me – the people tellin' you such hateful things about me –

WALLACE. Oh this is rich –

CORNELIA. No – It – was an act of hope –

WALLACE. Aaagk – I am a patient man – a forgivin' man. I believe in turnin' the other cheek. Then you pull this CRAP!

CORNELIA. No! It was an act of love –

WALLACE. Oh you kill me –

CORNELIA. I just wanted to hear if you still loved me –

WALLACE. Are you crazy?!? No, now, I'm just askin', cause this is what a crazy woman'd do! Cause if you're crazy, you sure don't belong here – you oughta be locked up where you can get proper attention –

(She scoops up the tapes:)

CORNELIA. Take 'em. Here – I don't want 'em – I hate 'em. Dump 'em in the river – Pleaaaase – ! I didn't mean it – I never meant it – I swear I didn't mean it –

WALLACE. Don't you know, don't you get it: sayin you didn't mean it, doin' somethin' you didn't mean –

CORNELIA. BUT I DIDN'T MEAN IT – !

WALLACE. *(with bitter irony:)* Awe, Honey – Welcome to the club.

CORNELIA. *(a beat)* Punish me. Get mad at me. Just don't turn me away.

(WALLACE *picks up the phone and punches three buttons:)*

WALLACE. This is the Governor. On the matter involving Mrs. Wallace? It is my instruction that all materials relating to this incident be destroyed – files, tapes, reports. That is correct.

(He hangs up.)

CORNELIA. *(heartfelt tears, touching his cheek:)* Thank you.

WALLACE. *(thundering:)* GET OUT OF MY SIGHT!! GET OUTTTTT!!!

(Pause. She crosses and sits on the bed, removing her stockings:)

WALLACE. What are you doin?

CORNELIA. I'm tired and I'm goin' to bed.

WALLACE. It's over. Pack a bag.

CORNELIA. No! Now just – No. And that's absolute final.

WALLACE. I said pack a bag. You can come 'round later for the rest of your things –

CORNELIA. *(steely:)* No, I won't – !

(Almost gay:)

– Or maybe I will, teach you a lesson – better shape up now, mind your Ps and Qs –

WALLACE. Don't you be goin' crazy on me –

CORNELIA. *(abruptly, peevish:)* I only did what I had to do, and I didn't do anything you didn't do, and just cause you're throwing in the towel doesn't mean I am –

WALLACE. Cornelia –

CORNELIA. You stayin' up later or not?

WALLACE. Goddamn, I am warning you –

CORNELIA. Well don't! Maybe I've got more tapes. Tons more.

WALLACE. Oh don't you threaten me –

CORNELIA. I hid 'em! I'm not foolin' around so just – Don't – This is our bedroom, our home! I am First Lady and I am your wife. I am George Wallace's secret weapon. I am beautiful, brainy, a needed touch of class to the Wallace effort. Tomorrow you'll see this is just a little bump in the road – There's not a single reason we can't put this behind us – Tomorrow everything'll be just up, up and away.

WALLACE. Get out of that bed – I mean it, get out of that bed!

(Lights rise in intensity as **WALLACE** *wheels toward the bed, then lunges for* **CORNELIA**'s *foot. She resists.)*

CORNELIA. NO! Let me go – Let me go!!!

(Spits, hissing:)

YOU leave! Why am I always the one who has to leave?! YOU get out! You see what it feels like!! This is our home – I am not leaving – I am never leaving – !!

*(***WALLACE** *pulls her to the floor.)*

NOOOOOOOOOOOOOOOOOO – !!

(a beat)

*(***CORNELIA** *rises then slowly separates from tableau. As she steps back to narrator's position, lights fade on the bedrooom.)*

(Smoke and fog slowly envelop the stage.)

He kept an unsigned divorce petition in his drawer that entire last month. I used to check it every morning to

see if I was still married. Someone tipped off Channel f
our and they found a copy hidden under the bell pep-
pers at the Winn Dixie. Two days after that – he signed
it. And I left the man who cried in my arms and called
me Mama. And I left the house I grew up in forever.

*(Softly, building, the Cars' "Drive" plays in back-
ground.***)*

CORNELIA. *(cont.)* He lived on for years and years. Alone. A
long, slow fade from the spotlight. Bedridden. Stone
deaf. Dinky little place over on Perry. After all the millions that passed through his campaign treasury – he
never took a penny. Poor George. Sometimes, you
want a dream too badly, you destroy it. Sometimes, you
want it too badly, it destroys you.

(beat)

And me? Oh, I've had no permanent mailing address
for a few years now. Eighteen, to be exact. I purchase my
clothes at thrift shops. Been on welfare for – a stretch.
Guess it's my wanderin' in the woods phase. The Lord's
lookin' out for me. Not much. But a little.

(reassuring:)

Oh I really am okay. And I do like it here. The grounds
are gorgeous and quite well maintained. All my doctors
treat me well. And it's quiet. Mmm, I like that. I can
really think straight. You know? Figure out what's what,
what's really important. And all the rest – just – let it go.

(ruefully)

A Wallace and a Folsom. My rendevous with destiny.

(long pause, then a sly smile:)

It's just that – Thing is –

(half beat)

We still talk. At night. Alone in the Mansion. I call out.
He hears me.

(softly)

*** Please see Music Use Note on Page 3.

Darlin – ?

(a beat, then grins:)

Y'all think I'm crazy as a loon.

(A spot finds **WALLACE** *in his wheelchair, old and decrepit in the fog.)*

(long pause)

WALLACE. Cornelia – ?

(A look of confirmation on her face.)

(Blackout)

End of Play

OTHER TITLES AVAILABLE FROM SAMUEL FRENCH

NOVEMBER

David Mamet

Full Length, Comedy / 4m, 1f

David Mamet's new Oval Office satire depicts one day in the life of a beleaguered American commander-in-chief.

It's November in a Presidential election year, and incumbent Charles Smith's chances for reelection are looking grim. Approval ratings are down, his money's running out, and nuclear war might be imminent. Though his staff has thrown in the towel and his wife has begun to prepare for her post-White House life, Chuck isn't ready to give up just yet. Amidst the biggest fight of his political career, the President has to find time to pardon a couple of turkeys — saving them from the slaughter before Thanksgiving — and this simple PR event inspires Smith to risk it all in attempt to win back public support. With Mamet's characteristic no-holds-barred style, *November* is a scathingly hilarious take on the state of America today and the lengths to which people will go to win.

"Ferociously original…and crisply performed, [*November*] rollicks from one politically incorrect punch line to the next."
– *San Francisco Chronicle*

"Savage merriment…delightful…wild…brilliant"
– *San Francisco Examiner*

"Vaudeville meets current events…David Mamet just couldn't resist the bully pulpit of satire."
– *San Jose Mercury News*

"Remarkable…one of the most profoundly laugh-out-loud plays that I have seen in many years."
– *BeyondChron.org*

OTHER TITLES AVAILABLE FROM SAMUEL FRENCH

APHRODISIAC

Rob Handel

Drama / 1m, 2f

Congressman Dan Ferris is being questioned about the disappearance of intern Ilona Waxman. Sound awkward? Imagine if he was your dad...

"A genuine thrill ride. As dizzying as a Nabokov-written episode of *The West Wing*."
–The New York Sun

"Handel intelligently weaves together the threads of the story, and the characters shift voices and perspectives with little or no advanced warning...This lends much of the dialogue a witty, unpredictable texture..."
–talkinbroadway.com

"A cynical black comedy that's bathed in a kind of playfulness."
–Denver Post